MORE PRAISE FOR *PERMISSION*

'An intimate study of power within two of the relationships that define us most precisely – that of lover and that of child.'

– *Kirkus Reviews*

'In her elegant and compelling debut novel, the American writer Saskia Vogel sets about taking down the patriarchy, the Hollywood dream machine and the prejudices against people who are into BDSM.' – *The Irish Times*

'[*Permission*] pairs familial love and loss with erotic desire, creating a tempting, quick-paced, emotionally charged novel… The descriptions of sex and desire that follow are also impeccable… *Permission* layers kink into the human, everyday feelings of desire and loss, normalizing and personifying it.'

– Laura Winnick, Broadly

'Formidable in its elegance and fierce in its simplicity, Saskia Vogel's writing leaves the reader stunned and moved and wanting more. *Permission* is a work of subtle psychological skill that breaks down the negotiations of erotic power; it is also a work of great and surprising tenderness. '

– Andrea Scrima, author of *A Lesser Day*

'Part *Day of the Locust*, part *Story of O*, Vogel's unflinching, tender debut is destined to enter the growing canon of great Los Angeles novels.' – Ryan Ruby, author of *The Zero and the One*

'If Joan Didion had written about the BDSM community in L.A. it may have felt a bit like Permission, Saskia Vogel's evocative debut novel.' – John Freeman, LitHub

PERMISSION

BY
SASKIA VOGEL

COACH HOUSE BOOKS | TORONTO

first edition

LIBRARY AND ARCHIVES CANADA CATALOGUING IN PUBLICATION

Title: Permission / by Saskia Vogel.
Names: Vogel, Saskia, author.
Identifiers: Canadiana (print) 20190052902 | Canadiana (ebook) 20190052910 | ISBN 9781552453803 (softcover) | ISBN 9781770565814 (EPUB) | ISBN 9781770565821 (PDF)
Classification: LCC PS3622.O357 P47 2019 | DDC 813/.6—dc23

Permission is available as an ebook: ISBN 978 1 77056 581 4 (EPUB), ISBN 978 1 77056 582 1 (PDF)

Purchase of the print version of this book entitles you to a free digital copy. To claim your ebook of this title, please email sales@chbooks.com with proof of purchase. (Coach House Books reserves the right to terminate the free digital download offer at any time.)

'I am a pornographer. From earliest childhood,
I saw sex suffusing the world.'
– Camille Paglia

Last night I couldn't sleep, so I went for a drive. I only meant to take a loop around the peninsula, driving up and down the hills, seeing the city to the north, the port to the west, and the Pacific Ocean reaching for the dark horizon. It was just past midnight, so I tuned in to a rock station that had a late-night call-in show about sex and relationships. It had been on the air as long as I could remember, since before I'd thought of doing anything more than holding hands. It was the kind of show that made driving bearable. Once you've learned the words to every song on the radio, nothing breaks the boredom of sitting behind the wheel like conversation. Nervous callers made themselves vulnerable to a psychologist who'd heard it all before. He did his best to help, assuring people that they were not alone in fear, confusion, or desire. Whatever it was they wanted, they were allowed, he said, so long as it was safe, sane, and consensual. There was one thing he'd ask that made me bristle. Whenever a girl called in with a problem, he'd start off by asking, 'Where's Dad?' Where's Dad? As if that were the key to it all.

ECHO

THE HILLS WERE SLEEPING GIANTS, twitching as they dreamed. Each time they rolled over in their beds, maintenance crews arrived to fix the cracks in the coastal road, and the sea sucked stones from the shore. When the hills caught fire during the dry season, I stood at the cliffs watching helicopters lower their buckets into the water. I'd search for the pilot's eyes as the chopper rose into the sky, up and over my parents' house, hoping they were carrying nothing but water. Brush fire and broken roads were everyday dangers, like rattlesnakes and car crashes. I kept a packed suitcase in my closet, should the earth shake or fire jump the road. Even as a child, I knew the landscape would not hold.

The landscape brought other fascinations to my family's front door. We would watch migrating whales logging or lunging in the coves. We spent the season counting and took our tallies to the interpretive centre, a squat building next to a lighthouse surrounded by a garden of native plants. Through Bakelite handsets, I listened to underwater recordings of whales, their haunted songs, their hearts. In the long silence between each slow beat, I'd take my pulse. I often returned to this quiet space, finding relief in the cocoon of a steady, even bass.

In another room, dioramas depicted centuries of cliff erosion in the area. Fifty feet, one hundred feet, gone. The present-day model showed the cliffs as they were. Nothing had crumbled in a long while, even in the landslide zones. But I knew what that meant. A crumbling was overdue. Before I grew old, the land would claim our bodies and we would rise again as ghosts. Ghosts, like the young woman who haunted the lighthouse. She had thrown herself off these cliffs when she was sure her sailor would never return. She entered oblivion to find him. It was the most romantic story I knew. I liked to imagine love's oblivion. A yielding of the self to sensation, a sensation that belonged to the nights I fell asleep with my hands cupped between my legs, comforted.

On these nights, I was sure I could hear the lovers' laughter rising from the waves. Their joy beckoned. Once I followed the sound to the end of the garden, through the fence and to the cliff, crawling under the rail, inching closer and closer, closer to the edge than I'd ever dared. Peering down the wall of sedimentary rock, I discovered a ledge. Huddled figures wrapped in a cloud of something cloying, like roses wilting in a bowl. Laughing as if their rock were the only rock that promised never to fall. *Fall, fall, fall,* the cliffs whispered. *Dear God, If I fall, please let me die on impact.* Paralysis would be worse than death, I thought, and it frightened me. I couldn't imagine myself without this body, even though as a child I sensed its limits, the built-in obsolescence. The call grew louder, and eventually I stopped taking walks along the cliffs.

By the time I was ten, my father had had enough of my living in fear. He said it was not death that awaited me at the foot of the cliffs, but a beach. I could get anywhere, as long as I knew how to navigate my environment. I think he grew to like those cliffs so much because the longer we spent in that house, the less he seemed to be able to keep a grasp on us, especially on my mother, whose refusal to be pleased was a form of tyranny. The cliffs he could handle. Scaling the sedimentary rock, sliding down a steep and sandy path, he taught me about footholds and grips and how to read the stones. The sea at our feet, indifferent to us. It was a rocky beach, not suitable for swimming or sunbathing, most easily accessed by boat. On the shore: tide pools, sunbaked kelp, seal carcasses, cans eaten by the salty air, weather-beaten dirty magazines, traces of fire. I pictured the molten glow of midnight fisherman roasting their catch, wary of the siren's song. Even the air on the beach was sticky.

I would linger by the spreads of nude women bleaching in the sun. That pleasing tension, the muscular contraction of the sea cucumber, the gentle suction of an anemone's tentacles when I stuck my finger in the water, pretending I was a clownfish, impervious to its sting.

Rusty kelp beds broke the blue, red markers bobbed above where fisherman laid their traps. Down the crescent of our cove, my father and I scaled the lip of its rocky maw. When low tide turned to high, frothy waves crashed against the throat of the cave, and when they receded, they licked the pebbled floor clean. The first time I saw the cave and the rocky point, I refused to follow him across.

'Don't be scared,' he said. 'Just don't fall.'

Fifteen years we climbed over that cave.

And then, one day, he fell.

I didn't see it happen. He was ahead of me, and then he wasn't. That's what I told emergency services. There was a response boat. Helicopter. Harbour Patrol. Divers. They were out on the water until morning. We were told they'd stay in 'search-and-rescue mode' until 'the victim' was found. After the twenty-four-hour mark, they started to call it 'body recovery,' but even that search failed. I asked them what they were calling it now, but they would give no answer. They started passing the buck, each one telling me to ask another department.

In the aftermath, I spent most of my days at home with my hands pressed to the large glass panes facing our clear ocean view. When I had spent so long looking I could no longer tell sea from sky, my hands stayed put on the windowpane, feeling every vibration, every thud of wind. I was still in the womb when the shipping company they worked for moved my parents from Rotterdam to Los Angeles, but I was old enough to remember when they built it. Their dream home. How carefully they chose each detail, the joy they were able to take in it and each other. I didn't understand why we needed to leave the small house with the floral wallpaper by the port, where we could see cranes unloading containers from cargo ships, and every day at dusk a man who skateboarded around the neighbourhood with a trumpet under his arm stopped to play 'Taps.' But when I first saw the house, it was unreal.

A great white box planted atop a bluff, a jut of land pushing into the sea, set apart from every other house on the street. Instead of sirens and trumpets, we heard peacocks and seals. The house was glass and steel and full of light. Once inside, you could see the ocean from just about any angle. At sunset the walls turned tangerine, then violet, before darkness arrived and gave us the stars. 'Every day a love letter,' my father would say, my mother in his arms, taking in the life they had built together. I preferred to think of them like this. Optimistic, trusting in whatever logic kept them from getting a divorce.

Standing at that same window, it wasn't the ocean I saw but seams: silicone, grout, hinges, and brackets. All that was holding the house together and all the ways in which it could fall apart. Cracked Malibu tiles in the entryway, cracks running down the stucco walls. I inspected the silicone that held our kitchen sink in place, the build-up in the corners, the way the basin never really dried. Corrosion. I took the trash cans out of the cabinet under the sink and ran my fingers along the scar-like material holding it in place, feeling for edges that had unstuck themselves. Testing their integrity with my thumbnail, feeling sick when it slid underneath.

After my father disappeared, the Friday of Memorial Day weekend, my mother forgot to cancel the barbecue, which made for awkward conversations at the door. We didn't invite anyone in but the caterer. I unplugged the phone. There was no reason for me to go back to my apartment in the city after the holiday weekend, so I waited a while, subsuming myself in her rhythm of sleep and reheated macaroni, marinated meat, and booze. The caterer had packed everything into single servings, some for the freezer, some for the fridge. *You'll need to eat*, she kept saying. My mother split each serving in half, and when she handed me my plate she would say, *This is no excuse to let ourselves go*. Blanca cleaned up after us and made sure there was fresh milk for my father, as usual. After the milk went sour, Blanca asked where Mr. Jack was and my mother told her that he'd be back, but she must have asked around the neighbourhood because I heard her crying in the laundry room.

During these days, his absence led to a kind of ease between my mother and me, but we still didn't find a way into conversation. What was there to say? He might still return. And when I thought, no, maybe he's really gone, it wasn't words that wanted to come out of my mouth, but screaming. Finger-pointing and blame. And if I started in on blame, I was afraid of what she would say. I would blame her for pushing him away, and she would point to my fear as the cause of his demise. When we'd exhausted each other, maybe we'd cry together, talk about the loss of a man who'd never been good at making room for us in his life. All of it was too much and too unpredictable. It was best to keep my mouth shut and wait.

Each night, we sat on the balcony and stared at the ocean. Each night, she'd go to the pantry and take out one cigarette from the ceramic jar marked 'garlic.' She'd drop the ash into a wet paper towel and toss the sooty lump in the trash can in the garage. She left no trace because she promised him she'd quit. One morning I woke to find an ashtray on the kitchen table and stale smoke in the air. I never loved her less than I did then.

It seems inevitable in the retelling. My mother and father playing house, building their lives and their love in the shape of something familiar, never stopping to question the structure, the structure not being able to hold. But really, I don't remember much about those early weeks after he fell, how it went and why, apart from the forgetfulness – going to get milk from the kitchen but only managing to take a glass from the cupboard before being distracted by something else, and finding myself in another room wondering what the glass was doing in my hand. The crying that kept me from sleep, the thoughts that wouldn't quit, guilt, resentment, the gape of loss. Day after day passed by, then June was over and I was still at my parents' house. It's easy to lose track of time in Los Angeles even when you're not wondering where Dad is, whether gone means gone and what being gone means. The sun and sky are narcotic. Seventy-five degrees and clear afternoon skies by the beaches day after day after day.

THE FORTUNE TELLER SAW all of this coming. Or maybe her words were what had set my fears in motion so they could exert their force on the world. Sometimes I think if she had said something else, I'd be a different person now. You have to be careful with what you tell children. It sticks.

I met her right before my parents 'took a break,' a trial separation that would last only a few months. I was seven, maybe eight, already braced for change. Maybe it had something to do with the environmental education we had at school, which instilled a fear of unstable ground and the water running out. Some kids might have walked away with lessons on conservation, but me, I lost trust that anything could ever last. I was forever waiting for tragedy.

Like every year, the interpretive centre hosted a whale-watching jamboree. Crowds leaned their weight on the railing that ran along the cliff, trusting it to hold them, binoculars pressed to their eyes, scanning the sea for spouts and tails. Kids from my school were shoving their hands in bags of cotton candy and playing Pin-the-Tale-on-the-Whale as though it couldn't have been any other way. I wanted to know how long we had before it would be all over. Before all this sun and sea and rock came to its end.

The morning of the jamboree, my parents had been fighting again. They'd been fighting so long they seemed to forget I was there, ready to get in the car, ready to watch for whales. They shouted their competing interests at each other, something about how my father preferred to spend his Sunday. He wanted alone time; my mother said that weekends were for family, and the jamboree had been in our shared calendar for weeks. He insisted that everything he did was for the family, and he needed one damn minute for himself. He punctuated his rage with the words 'If that's all right with you, *dear*.' *Dear*: cold and slithering with sarcasm. I hadn't known a term of endearment could be weaponized until then. My mother didn't say anything after that. He took his car and 'went for a drive,' and I ended up alone with my mother at the jamboree. It was a sombre affair. She kept dabbing at her eyes under her sunglasses and disappearing with other moms while I threw darts at balloons.

Beyond the stalls selling windbreakers covered in puffy paint, I saw a purple tent shimmering off the main drag. The clapboard sign featured a crystal ball and stars. I imagined a sea witch who'd lost her seat in Poseidon's court but whose dark magic was still at work. I was sure she was there for me. I begged my mother for the entirety of my week's allowance so the fortune teller could tell me that this storm was not going to tear my family apart, that it would pass, as others had.

After the fights they'd had before their separation, they'd sit me down and say: *Just because we fight, it doesn't mean we don't love each other. We get under each other's skin because we love each other so much.* Their rough patch seemed to last so long I came to understand my father's absence from my everyday life, even when he was right there at home putting out fires on the phone during dinner, as an act of love. In a way it was. He was taking care of us. And as he liked to remind my mother, there was no *this*, he'd gesture around the house, without *this*, the ringing phone and files under his arm. My mother wanted his time, she said. But they could never agree on how to spend it. She liked to plan, he liked to see where the day would take him. Only after I met Orly and understood that loving in the way you love is not enough – you have to pay attention to how people need and want to be loved – did I come to realize that they were blind to each other.

As a child, I couldn't figure out how a story like theirs could turn out so rotten. It had sounded like the stuff of old romantic comedies with fast-talking, strong-minded women, and men who get the girl in the end. My father, the businessman abroad. My mother, his peer, at first mistaken for his secretary. A battle of wills that became a battle for her heart. I thought the fact that I was here meant that theirs was a happy ending. But if a happy ending looked like this, then I needed a love that was greater than theirs. All would be well with a love like that.

Inside the fortune teller's tent, it was stuffy and hot but for the breeze working its way into my jelly sandals. Across the table, the fortune teller asked for my hand. She studied my lines. I studied hers. The crescents of her nails, the crescent moons hung from her ears and neck. Her eyelids, turquoise demilunes.

She said: 'When other people fall, they can get right back up, dust themselves off, and keep going. Not you. You break. And you have to figure out how to put yourself back together each time.'

I pulled my hand away.

'It's what I see,' she said.

I never asked about my future again.

The fortune teller could have put it differently: you're a sensitive person; you'll need a thick skin. Then I might have cultivated a callus. Instead, I tried not to break, moving through the world without friction, following the path laid out before me. I'd do well in school, I'd curl my hair and make sure my face was done, ever ready for love's arrival. Love would be my salvation and the force against which my character would be formed. I suppose that's how I got into acting, to get an idea of some of the many selves I might become once taken in by love's power. I liked trying on these other lives, stretching each new role over me, covering the fractures inside.

My first audition was for an innovative yogurt product designed for women on the go. I mean, they were basically large ketchup packets filled with fruit-flavored yogurt that you sucked down, no need for a spoon. It was right before my senior year of high school. The casting agent who'd visited my summer drama program called right after the audition to tell me that I was exactly what they wanted: a fresh face for a fresh product with a major national roll-out. Nothing had ever felt so good. I was young, but I wasn't getting any younger. I didn't want to end up like Linda.

Linda was my mother's friend from the shipping company. Unlike my mother, she had kept her job and would visit sometimes when she was in town for business. I remember her copper-red hair and eyes like Cleopatra, the way she smoked and touched my dad on the knee when she addressed him. How the touch made him nervous. I think my mom liked watching him squirm, having something over him.

Linda must have been around fifty and me a teenager when I saw her last, same hair and makeup, same hand on the knee. My father seemed to enjoy her just as much. After dinner, he and Linda left the table to finish the wine on the balcony, and as my mom and I cleaned up the kitchen, she asked if I didn't think it was about time Linda retired the femme fatale act. I remember dutifully agreeing with her that Linda, the way she was at her age, was tragic. But this agreement settled inside me as a seed of agitation. I couldn't stop thinking about it. I liked seeing Dad happy and relaxed. And I liked Linda. There was so much to her: energy, conviction, and mystery. A lightness my mother did not have. A certain style. In Linda, I saw a woman capable of giving and receiving joy, and the effect it had on my dad. Until then, I'd thought my mother's dissatisfaction was noble and luxurious: it meant her life was full enough for her to be dismissive of its bounty. I thought my mother's capacity for displeasure was a sign that she was discerning.

My yogurt commercial was still on the air around the Christmas holidays, when everyone else at school was awaiting decisions on their college applications. But I was ahead of the game. I had a career, so I kept at it and stayed in the Los Angeles area long after most of my classmates moved away. I had a good run. Five years where I was exactly what they wanted, but then whatever shine I'd had dulled, and by the time I entered my mid-twenties, I wasn't what anyone wanted anymore. All I'd been hearing before my agent dropped me was, 'They couldn't see you in the part.' I knew exactly what they meant. I was surprised it had taken them so long to catch on. I'd never been passionate about acting, I'd just gotten into a groove. But the last real role I'd had was two years ago. I played 'Young Camp Counsellor' in a reboot of a nineties show about rich high school kids. It was a three-episode arc. I had a few lines. And after those few days up in Malibu, where I mostly hung out in the shade with the rest of the cast, trading stories about life in the canyons – people who got lost, mountain lions, and secret pot farms – I had a decent year's salary. Enough to make me want to do better, but still enough to not worry about making too much of an effort. I can't tell you how I spent my time. I read. I treated dating like it was my job. The men were easy fun. There was more to it, of course, but I liked the customs that came with being a woman on a date with a man. I was well-rehearsed. Women gave me stage fright. With women, there was an open space of possibility, a potential to define the relationship on our terms, but that meant I had to account for myself. After Ana, I was afraid of being hurt. And behind that fear was that wish for love, for sensation, the dreams I dreamt in the silence between two heartbeats.

As for acting, I guess I'd hoped I could keep doing what I'd been doing. But since 'Young Camp Counsellor,' I hadn't booked anything of consequence. In the past two years, I played the lead in a student feature, helped out behind the scenes on other people's passion projects, and danced in a music video privately funded by a musician I'd been sleeping with off and on for a few months. He was beautiful, and our bodies were better in conversation than we were, which was its own kind of rare.

To keep myself going, I'd been doing odd jobs. For a while I was earning enough serving drinks, snacks, and views of my ass at a monthly poker party at a private residence off Mulholland. The tips were good if you could just be a body in a tight uniform. The host said there was more work if I wanted it. Did I have a business suit? I did. It had been a graduation gift from my mother, because 'everyone needs one someday,' which was really her way of telling me that I was chasing a pipe dream.

'Here's the deal,' the party's host said. 'You come over for a "meeting" when my wife is home. Briefcase, files, office-appropriate shoes, tasteful jewellery and makeup. The whole deal. Business formal. And then we fuck on my desk. Fifteen hundred bucks. You're in and out in an hour.'

One of the other girls I worked with ended up taking the gig, but I don't know – after I turned him down, something changed. What had felt like fast cash for doing little more than showing up and being friendly turned sour. There was something in the way he'd claimed me with his offer. And how he started to resent me when I didn't indulge his advances, even though the woman I became at those events had always played hard to get. His breath on my neck against the pantry door when I was restocking the nuts. How satisfied he sounded with himself when he called me *incorrigible*. I wasn't planning on going back after Memorial Day, and I'd been looking forward to the long weekend with my dad to think things through. Dad didn't need to know the details, though telling him would have probably meant he'd slip me a few months' expenses. He was like that with gifts, haphazard and practical. He'd never have given me a dime if I asked for it straight out. All I wanted that Memorial Day weekend was to pick his business brain. He was good at being dispassionate, catching loose strands and weaving them into a plan. I wanted a plan, some sort of structure. But then he was gone.

IN THOSE BLANK WEEKS of sorrow, it fell to me to keep our fridge stocked. After we had worked our way through the barbecue food from the caterer, I thought I'd start working my way through the pantry, but I couldn't bring myself to touch any of it, not even a half-eaten bag of tortilla chips kept closed with an ancient rubber band, the kind that my dad had around his file folders when they got thick. I couldn't bring myself to take that rubber band off. It was stretched out and brittle, and if it broke, I'd have to go through the drawer under the telephone in the kitchen where all the rubber bands, binder clips, and freebie pens ended up. The junk of life, the stuff you think you're going to organize one day. The very thought of the drawer made me feel unstable. Disturbing anything that was his felt dangerous. So, I kept the door to the pantry shut and filled my time with going to the grocery store. It was, at least, a way to force myself to shower, and because of the distances in this city, a fantastic way of killing time. Some days, I made sure to leave the house when the schools let out, and I'd take the road that always got clogged with moms and minivans so I could sit in traffic, the sun in my face, the radio on, and wait for a flash of how things used to be.

When I'd moved to my apartment in the city, I'd taken what I needed and tossed all the things I didn't, so my childhood bedroom didn't have much in it. I borrowed my mother's clothes: capri pants, leather sandals, and a twinset. The door to my father's closet was closed, and only once did I slide the door open a crack and sniff. The air was stale but thick with him, and I thought I might be sick. I shut the door.

I would let my long hair air dry in the wind as I drove those miles to the shopping mall, with the windows rolled down. Except for my tangled hair, I looked like every mom around. My mother's clothes smelled of carnal white florals. And sometimes I saw her feet in the coral shoes, her legs in the pale-blue trousers, which were just shy of being too tight on me. As my mother liked to point out, I'd inherited my father's bones. It made me think she was disappointed in me, but the feeling was mutual. I might have thick bones, but what kind of life had she given in to?

I would push the cart around the grocery store and keep my sunglasses on. I wanted something between me and the world, a different surface for the world to interact with, so I could be left to my sadness. Not only sadness but a poisoned feeling, like there was something wrong with the groundwater and I had to keep it away from my skin. I hoped I wouldn't run into anyone I knew. In a community as small as ours, anyone I went to school with would know me by my walk, the back of my ear.

Neither my mother nor I had it in us to cook. Our freezer had been full of casseroles that had been dropped off at our house like offerings to an angry god, but this had now stopped, as though there were an expiration date on sympathy. I took the end of these gestures as a judgment: the first swell of grief should have passed by now, the absent dishes seemed to say. From the deli counter, I bought concoctions for which my dad used the umbrella term 'salad' and that never seemed to spoil. Foods like those the caterer had brought for the barbecue, as if by stocking the fridge just so, I could live that day again. This time he wouldn't fall.

If the counter was out of potato salad, my throat would close up and my sinuses would swell. I'd go straight to the checkout, grab a roll of mints and crunch my way through the packet, the menthol clearing my nasal passages. Even in those fits of despair, there was value in my shopping routine. When our pantry and fridge were full, I still did my rounds of the aisles. My mother was either asleep, busy with the people who administrate death, or on the phone with relatives overseas. The one time she handed me the phone, I could just about manage to speak German to my cousin. My cousin and I didn't know each other well so our exchange was short, dutiful, and polite. My shopping routine gave me something of my own in those weeks. And it was during these trips, as I pulled in and out of our driveway, that I began to notice the men.

Initially, I thought the men were one man in particular: the old neighbour across the street, a retired longshoreman who split his time between Alaska and Hawaii. But I didn't recognize him. Maybe it was a brother or a cousin. Workmen, I thought one day when there was a truck outside packed with lumber and shopping bags from the home improvement store. There was a man my father's age with a ponytail who carried the lumber in, and a petite man who walked with a self-conscious shuffle. The first time I saw the builder's car on the curb outside the neighbour's house, I parked on our driveway at an angle that allowed me to watch him in my rear-view mirror. He did things that Dad used to do: home improvement projects that involved tarp, tools, plants, and wood. He left orange buckets filled with gloves and paint rollers on the driveway, which the smaller man would rearrange behind the pygmy palms flanking the entryway, so the mess was less visible from the street. Surely, I thought, there must have been more to my father than home improvement, but every attempt at memory felt contrived. My memories could have been the memory of many dads, I thought. Had I already forgotten what had made him mine? One day when she found me crying, Blanca held me and told me that Mr. Jack was a good man, he worked hard and loved his family very much. In that moment, her words were everything, but when I repeated them to myself they were just other words. I watched the builder and the petite man install a trellis at the front of the house, and together they planted jasmine and honeysuckle. The next day the builder and his truck were gone. The front door was open, and I heard hammering and drilling and the drone of a vacuum cleaner. One day, as I was driving off, I thought I saw the petite man wave.

I assumed the hybrid car in the driveway belonged to him, but I hadn't seen anyone driving it, though I did see other cars and other men. Their comings and goings caused an uncommon amount of traffic for our street, but it was really only noticeable if you spent as much time staring at the street as I did. The more strange cars I saw, the more I kept watch. The men flowed into the house. I imagined them accumulating there, like fish attracted by the algae and other life forms found on wharf pilings. A house crowded with men who built, carried file folders, made phone calls, fell asleep to the Weather Channel. What gravity had drawn these men here, what had tugged at their souls? I would catch myself thinking that my daddy would soon be drawn here, too. I looked for him in every man who came to the neighbour's door and found him every time: the waves had turned him old, or young, or sometimes bald. The depths of the ocean had compacted him. The moon's pull had stretched him long, and there he was, transformed, knocking at my neighbour's door. I thought about the moon at work on the tides, and I wished for its gravity to remake me too as I drove across the peninsula. When I parked at the shopping mall, I'd catch my reflection in the mirror, disappointed it was still me. I searched my image for his bones, but all I saw were my mother's keen eyes, her disappointment with our life.

I sat on the benches and watched mothers pick up birthday cakes from the baker my mother used, children being ferried to and from karate, sitting with nannies at the ice-cream parlour doing homework, mothers clutching yoga mats and coffees, fumbling with their handbags as the sun pounded the hoods of their polished cars. I watched other women whose lives were not mine. Sometimes I saw older girls I remembered from school, married with kids and running errands. I remembered how hard they'd tried to get into college, how focused they were on achieving. Girls who'd expended all that energy just to end up right back here. Look how they fit in. Theirs was the life that had been mine for the taking. I had my apartment and a life up in the city, almost an hour's drive away, but seeing them, even that didn't seem like enough distance, because here I was again. I never said hi.

Toward the end of June I spotted a flyer from the community art centre on the noticeboard at the grocery store. It was pinned near want ads for dog-walkers, cleaners, and people offering bodywork, horse-back riding, and Mandarin lessons. The thought of interacting with kids or dogs or families drove me to tears. I wouldn't be able to control my tongue, and yet I didn't want to talk about my father. I knew what words could conjure, and I wasn't ready to be a fatherless child. But seeing that familiar logo made me smile. Ana and I had taken drawing classes there, sometimes with our mothers, and those were happy times. The art centre was looking for models. The pay was good, but not like the poker party: it was regular-pay good. I needed to do more than shopping and liked the idea of having a job where I didn't have to say a word.

THE MODEL FOR THE SCULPTING workshop had cancelled her bookings last minute, so I had a gig for the next month if I wanted one, Fumiko, the instructor, told me on the phone. The students had already built their armatures and needed a female figure to work from. All I had to do was show up five minutes before class and bring a robe. On Wednesday evening, I drove to the top of the peninsula. I took my place on the model stand, took Fumiko's instruction, and dropped my robe when she said it was time.

I didn't notice him right away. He was outside my field of vision and I was busy practicing a technique I'd learned in an acting class, relaxing my body so that it was working with gravity instead of against it. But with acting, you were in motion. A few minutes in, I could already feel the strain in my hip where I was putting most of my weight. I was trying to keep my arches high and not sink into my heels, to make sure my ankles were balanced and toes relaxed. My raised arms were tingling. The coastal breeze had chased the heat off for the night and a low fog rested on the hills. A fan heater ticked to and fro, burning my calves when it swung my way. I counted the seconds until its return, because burning was better than the dim chill of the studio. I tried not to think of the tingling, ache, and cold as I monitored the timer's slow march from twenty to zero, but as my body began to sink, my position shifted enough to see who it was. His face was thinner than I remembered, but it was him. Ana's father, slicing through his block of clay with wire string, thick lumps dropping to the linoleum floor. I had to force myself to stay put. I had never wanted to see him again. And now here I was, legs on fire, nipples puckering, drafts catching in my pubic hair. Too aware of my skin, my blood. My body's refusal to be still – especially in front of him – seemed obscene. I focused on Fumiko. It was all I could do. I hoped no one could see how my body had begun to pound.

Fumiko was padding around the room, nodding at some, grunting commands at others and taking their hands in hers to correctly fit them around their tools, slicing at the edges, jamming her fingers into the clay to show what it means to make the hollow of an eye. At Ana's father's piece, Fumiko shook with what sounded like a dry cough. I kept my arms up and folded, but turned my head enough so I could see her. She was chuckling sweetly, as though she'd bumped into an old friend. She gave the flanks of his sculpture a hearty slap. She ran her hands over the mounds of clay that made up the breasts, then pinched off a protrusion that seemed to be a nipple and stuck it to his pedestal. The narrow waist was a bridge losing its fight to keep the mighty bosoms connected to the boulders of her ass. Of course his sculpture was confused. He didn't know how to see me.

Ana's father avoided looking at Fumiko until she gripped his wrist, and he made a nervous sound. 'We accentuate the things we find pleasing, but you have to give it a logical architecture. Look at her. Really look at her. It's why she's here.' To me, she said, 'Stand straight.' Then, 'Class,' she clapped her hands; her fingers left stains on his skin.

Fumiko demonstrated how to use your hand as a measuring tool. The men and women around me each raised an arm and held out their fists, some with their thumbs up, some to the side, others resting their thumbs against hard tools. Dr. Moradi and I locked eyes. I'd tried to hush the memory, but it would not be stilled.

Ana and me. The two of us, the summer before senior year. Afternoon sun in her curtains, hurried hands, too impatient to get undressed. At first the creak and rustle of the bed was everything, then it was hands and skin, the act of kissing, but also the sound, her hands in my hair and mine inside her. We didn't notice her door had been left ajar until it shut. She thought it was the wind. Then, we heard the rolling click of the lock. Ana froze. I said we should go out the window. When she didn't follow, when I heard her pleading with him, I started running. I shouldn't have run away without her, but I ran those few miles home.

Without looking up from the bills she was paying, my mother asked why I didn't call her if I wanted to leave early and wouldn't that be the day when I finally got my driver's licence. But then she must have heard it in my breath, maybe she could smell it on me. My T-shirt was dark with sweat and I had a blister on my foot. *Go take a bath*, she said. While I was in the tub, Moradi called. She came in without knocking, sat, and slid her hand through the bubbles. She looked spent and tender. *You'll take a break from each other over the summer, and I'm sure it will be back to normal by the time school starts*, she said and waited for a reply that didn't come. I was trying not to drown. The tap gurgled and water splashed into the bath. *We don't have to tell your father. If you don't want to.*

I didn't want to. There was nothing to say. We hadn't done anything we had been told not to do; I wasn't a boy. We were exploring, like what we had done when we were younger, practicing kissing on our pillows and hands. We didn't talk about what it meant. It was something we had always done, and we never stopped to question whether or not what we were doing was in anticipation of a man. I think about what my mother said next a lot. She may not have meant it the way I heard it, but it was in the ether. A stitch of judgment, a tic of abnormality, the threat of the Other to an ordered life.

You've never been one for the easy road, she said.

My mother thought she was lightening the mood, but instead I heard a suggestion about who I was, that what I wanted from Ana was not friendship, but love. And in my mother's face, her mildness, I understood the trouble desire could cause.

You can talk to me, my mother said, but though I believed her, it would be better for Ana if we all pretended this had never happened. My mother blew the bubbles off her fingers. They sailed between us like dandelion spores and sizzled when they landed on the foam.

Ana's parents had come to Los Angeles on vacation in the eighties, and it would be years until I understood what it actually meant for them to have decided right then never to go back to Iran. The Moradis had family up in Beverly Hills, but they didn't see each other often, and Ana had always said that her parents liked it that way, but something changed when the Beverly Hills uncle got ill. Suddenly, they were up there all the time at family gatherings, temple and, of course, the hospital. Ana had never talked about her bat mitzvah as anything other than a big birthday party and a chance to slow dance with Ryan Kim. We were still fondling our pillows then. But she'd started studying harder. I asked her about the effort she was putting into something neither she nor her parents believed in that much, and Ana replied, 'It's for my family,' and I knew she didn't mean just her parents. Instead of a birthday party, she started talking about becoming a woman, which to me seemed too distant to merit any serious thought. I didn't understand what had changed.

My parents didn't think about family like this. My dad said he was tired of being the one to always be going back home to Ohio, his siblings could come out here for a change, so we only saw them if there was a wedding or a funeral. My mother's parents were already gone, and she had no siblings. I admired Ana's reverence for something greater than herself. It made her seem protected, as though she could never come to harm because she had a world of people around her who cared. A bat mitzvah seemed like a small price to pay for that. What would it feel like to belong to something so self-evident, something you didn't give up on because you didn't feel like getting on a plane?

The summer break didn't have the palliative effect my mother had promised. But I gave her no reason to believe that time had not solved the problem, and she no longer asked me how I was or what I needed. I appreciated the privacy. 'I haven't seen Ana in a while,' my dad said one day. I pretended like I hadn't noticed, but he could tell there was more to it. He told me not to worry: people grow apart. I found myself thinking about her at night, her skin. I pushed those thoughts away, and when I masturbated, I pictured her with men. In my fantasies, I inhabited both bodies. I came, thinking about being filled.

That summer went by in a blur of hours. After the drama program ended, my mother made sure I 'kept busy' with 'activities.' These were words she associated with good kids and used them with a gusto reserved for people who feel ill at ease with language, but that was one thing I couldn't fault her for: English wasn't her mother tongue. Keeping busy meant that I spent any free day I had helping one of her friends who was renovating her stables. I couldn't stand the idea of our charity work for the mother-daughter assistance league; the risk of running into kids from my school, maybe Ana, was too high. So I brushed away the stable's cobwebs thick with yellow dust. I mucked the stalls. At the end of each day my skin was rubbery to the touch. No matter how I scrubbed I could still smell the sebum, manure, and wet hay.

My dad decided we should all drive down to Valle de Guadalupe for a week. It was the first vacation I could remember that wasn't also a business trip. He said he could tell we all needed a break. He taught me how to drink wine even though I was underage, and together we watched the sun gild the vineyards from the pool. It was nice. After dinner, I'd disappear to my room to read, falling asleep with my light still on, listening to them shush each other when they couldn't stop laughing. One day I didn't see them until dinner.

And then the school year started. I could tell my mother was relieved. She was tired of watching me 'mope around,' which seemed like a double standard. At least I looked like I was keeping busy with activities that resembled actual work.

But like the fortune teller said, I was no good at putting myself back together. Ana made other friends over the summer, kids whose parents were also from Iran and who went to the same synagogue. There was no room for me anymore, and because I still valued our friendship, I did what I thought she wanted me to do. I stayed away from her, but I didn't know where to go. Because we never finished what we started, because it never was allowed to reach a natural close, our ending felt unwritten. I imagined other endings and how they would have defined me, and because I couldn't explore such endings with her, my desire ran loose where it could. I responded to the desire of others, and I fell easily for those who responded to the desire in me. At times I felt worn thin, but it was exciting, and as I found out, rare to be a person who enjoyed both giving and receiving pleasure, who was interested in the erotic as an exchange. Some people couldn't see past the sex, some people fell fast and hard, and though I was generous with my body, I was careful and particular about whom I shared my heart with, and that left me lonely. People didn't think I was into relationships, and it became a self-fulfilling prophecy. Even so, the ability to participate in pleasure seemed to me to be the greatest good. In pleasure, differences fell away and made space for an ecstatic encounter during which the boundaries between us dissolved and we were free.

In their eyes, I was mostly a girl other girls could grind with, lips they could kiss, hair they could twist. This girl or that girl and whichever guys they were working their way through, guys who liked to think their dicks were magic or who approached me sweetly to find out if what they were doing was right. Right or wrong, I didn't know. In pleasure we were only bodies, and the body is all we have. This perspective wasn't without conflict. A woman I dated after I moved into my apartment had called me a pornographer because of it. She wanted emotional intimacy before we made love, and I told her I wanted to know what our bodies would be like together before I felt comfortable opening up. It was about trust and communication, I said, but she seemed insulted. I thought about the word *pornographer*. It suited me, in a way, but only because I knew of no better word for me yet. Sex was sacred to me. I knew it had the power to transform. In my arms, my lovers' eyes would roll back. Mouths opening, they'd offer me their tongues, their dreams and confessions. They came to me for comfort, they came for me, and each act was a conjuring spell. Just one more kiss, one more caress, I wished, and this body would be revealed to be hers. Why couldn't Dr. Moradi have let us be?

On the model stand, I fought back tears. All eyes were on me. They could see each quake. There was no place to hide. Fumiko spoke slowly, guiding them through how to break me down. She spread the jaws of the calipers and fitted them around my head. The metal tip on my skin, the unexpected touch, became a point of focus. I allowed it to become all that there was. One end pressed against the soft flesh covering the hollow of my jaw, the other at the crown of my head. The strange comfort of a touch that asked nothing of me. Fumiko had my full attention. There was no space for tears. She walked the apparatus up and down my body. Seven and a half heads high, three heads wide at the shoulders, and on and on, until she reached my feet.

'Good, good. Lucky class. She is classically proportioned,' Fumiko said when she was done. Standing among the students again, she said, 'Resume the pose.'

AS I DROVE HOME FROM the art centre that night, I thought about what I had left behind by leaving this suburb for the city. I was born into privilege and raised on narratives of success. But what my dad had called 'paradise' wasn't paradise to me. I couldn't understand how my parents didn't see it. I wasn't sure anyone who chose to live here did. In a newspaper article about a double-suicide that took place on the cliffs near our house while I was in high school, a mother from the neighbourhood asked to comment on the 'star-crossed lovers' said, 'You work so hard to give your kids everything, and they think it's hell.' It's as though she had forgotten how it felt to be in love, what it felt like to be left wanting. What it felt like when material comfort wasn't comfort enough. And yet, these values are deeply rooted. Sitting in my childhood home, I began to think of myself as a failure, losing sight of the value of the life I had chosen. Seeing Dr. Moradi made me feel like a loser, not least because I knew there was nothing he would have approved of about me now. He was exactly the kind of person who moved here. Or did the place shape him?

On this bulge of land at the edge of Los Angeles, Spanish, Craftsman, mid-century, and ranch-style homes lined winding roads with ocean views. The area had been conceived of as a beachfront retreat in the early twentieth century, beachfront with minimal beach access, for people who wanted to imagine they were beyond the reach of a hungrily expanding metropolis. Way back when, whiteness was the barrier for entry, but now it was only a certain level of success. Success meant money, and any way you earned it seemed fine. All money was moral, but not all fame, as the parents of my friends made clear with their contempt for the city where so many of them spent their days as lawyers and doctors and aerospace engineers. One of my father's concessions to my mother was that we'd live someplace where walking was possible. She couldn't have walked to the store, but there were miles of trails right outside our door. I suppose it was a sort of Eden: perfect only in the absence of knowledge from the outside. The people within its borders were trying to recreate places to which they wished to return. None of those places were real.

Unlike the rest of the city it was attached to, the peninsula was dark at night, a regulation intended to preserve the natural beauty of the place. The brightest lights were from passing cars, passing planes, fishing boats past midnight. But the darkness, its bends and corners, attracted a different kind of person, too. People who were out for a drive, who needed to be alone. For an area with good freeway access, it felt remote.

I was still thinking about this, surprised by the intensity of my resentment toward a place I thought I had simply left behind, when I pulled onto our driveway. The house was dark.

'Mom?' I called out when I came through the front door. I didn't want to spook her.

A sound came from the kitchen, a hissing inhalation that might have been a 'hello.' She gestured for me not to bother her. She was watching something out the window.

I opened the refrigerator and leaned into its cold air. Forks jutted from the plastic containers of creamy and fluffy mush. I had been telling myself I wasn't really eating, just picking at the peas and diced ham but not the mayonnaise-y macaroni. Mandarin wedges and pineapple but not the marshmallow. There was so much of that ambrosia, but I'd nearly whittled it down to the cream and carbohydrates. I picked up a fork and found a maraschino cherry still speared on the tines. I ate it. It was waxy, chilled and sickly sweet. I couldn't seem to get the sugar off my tongue. The fridge made a clicking sound and began to hum. I put the fork back in the bowl and closed the refrigerator door. I poured my mom and myself a glass of water and sat at the table with her, swishing the water around in my mouth, the sweetness diluted, then gone. When I stopped swishing, there were only waves and palms to be heard. They seemed to be growing louder each night.

We listened to the ocean pummel the shore. The phone rang. It went to voicemail. Telemarketer. After the initial shock, the missing, the waiting, there was nothing really to say. Maybe in silence we were understanding each other perfectly. Maybe silence was a respite we shared. I forgave her for smoking. Mom had her cigarettes, and I had my forks in the fridge. Nothing needed to be said, because we knew. We were in mourning, and it was OK to let our mourning be.

My mother sat up straighter.

I scooted my chair around and leaned over so I had a better view. She pointed at the last farm in the area. It wasn't much of a farm: passionfruit weighing down a rusted chain-link fence. Tomatoes and sunflowers. Leafy greens and strawberries. The farmer kept a trailer on the property, which stretched all the way to the sea and boasted the only passable road that led down to the beach. He'd come after you muttering, wielding something heavy or with a trigger if he caught you trespassing. I heard property developers were always trying to get him to sell, but the farmer must have been happy with what he was making renting out his access road to film crews. A picture truck was parked on the road, carrying something large on its bed.

One second we were looking at the truck, the next we were blinded by a bright, round light. A blue-flamed artificial sun. I had to look away. Chips of ash cast shadows on the kitchen table.

'They're shooting a major motion picture,' my mother said. 'That actress who looks like you is in it. What's her name?'

I didn't want to say it.

'Lola?'

I nodded.

'The location manager came by. Nice man. He seemed to worry that we would make a fuss. He invited us to drop by,' my mother said, sounding as if she thought it were that easy. A nice man came to your door, you had a nice chat and then you were invited to the set, as good as in. She always made it sound like everyone else knew how to do life better, it was just me who refused to walk down Easy Street. Try harder. Be better. Be nicer. Be more like Lola LaForce, who was basking in the same blue light, but being fawned over and paid.

'OK, I will,' I said, and started to get up, but then she put her soft hand on mine. The green eyes I'd inherited from her, suddenly sharp.

'Do. I want to know you're going to be OK…because…'

The water was rising inside her. She wiped fresh tears away.

I hugged her. She was stiff in my arms. I let her go. We were closer than we'd been in years.

There was discomfort in her smile. Her eyelids, angry swollen red. She fished a tube of hemorrhoid cream from the pocket of her silk robe, squeezed some out on her ring finger, the gentlest finger, and dabbed it around her eyes. Like she'd taught me. Her fingernails were perfect pale ovals. She hadn't even missed her fortnightly nail appointment at Janine's. I teared up at the sight of her rings. She was still wearing them.

Her diamonds, her nails, these things that were as they always were: I expected Dad to arrive at any second. The car would rumble up the driveway, the door to the garage would open and slam behind him. He'd want to go for a run before dinner but would decide he was too tired, pour himself a drink, sit on the balcony, and look at the view until dinner was ready. But it was well past dinnertime. And the keys to his car had disappeared along with him, so the convertible was gathering dust in the garage. My mother said she couldn't find the spare key. I couldn't bring myself to rummage through his hiding places. Surely, she knew them too. But it was enough to believe we'd find them one day. When we were ready to start looking. Maybe we'd look together, and she'd open up boxes of things I'd never seen and tell me stories about their marriage that I'd never heard. Ones that didn't end in pain or resentment.

My mother lit another cigarette.

'It's time to go home…' she said in her mother tongue.

To preserve whatever sense of camaraderie we had, I tried not to let on how her words hit me. I did my best to sound calm. I might not have understood her, after all.

'Haven't I been…' I started to say in English. She gave me one of her severe looks, her face all angles, just like mine. Disappointment, I thought, for not answering her in German.

'I've been thinking about Munich or maybe Lake Constance,' she finished.

She hated being interrupted, but there was nothing she liked more than making a plan, and the anticipation in the run-up, the *Vorfreude*. This was the best way I knew to apologize: 'We haven't been there since Omi died. Does your cousin still have the lake house?'

She tutted. 'Not for vacation.'

Mom kept talking. Telling me about her plans when the paperwork was done: life insurance and lease policies, transfer of ownership of his business. Paperwork to declare death in absentia. We seemed to have both decided not to bring up a memorial.

'Won't it take years?'

'It doesn't matter,' she said. 'The house is in my name.'

I stood at the end of the driveway with a baggie and pipe I'd made out of an apple. I'd found some dry pot from god-knows-when in my closet. It wasn't good, but it worked. I thought of it like a smudge stick, antiseptic and holy, driving the spirits from me: the what-ifs, the could-have-beens, the where-was-he-nows. I couldn't ask why because I would only blame myself: if I hadn't been so nervous as a child, if only I had been less afraid, he would never have been down there. I looked at my skin in the blue light from the film crew and played the air with my fingers. The shadows across the backs of my hands moved like light through water. I imagined pulling him to land.

The dinging of an open car door pierced the night. The sound was coming from the driveway across the road. It was coming from the hybrid. I waited to see the driver. For a second, I thought it might be my dad. Then I saw the silhouette of a woman. She put a box down on the driveway and faced the blue light, and then went back to unloading boxes. I forgot about the daddies. The arms of her T-shirt were cut-off, leaving her ribs exposed, and when she leaned into the car, the T-shirt shifted to show her breasts, small and high. Beautiful. Enviable. So unlike mine. She stopped and looked around. I wished for the cover of night, but she'd already seen me. The woman raised her hand in greeting, and I mirrored her gesture. There was something familiar about her. I was suddenly aware of my heart-beat, but also my cotton mouth.

She smiled and walked to the end of her driveway, across the street from mine.

'Hey,' she called out, as if we always talked like this. 'What's up with the light?'

But I couldn't speak. It took everything I had to say: 'Film crew.' The words left my mouth, and as they moved in her direction, they left a trail in the air.

'What?' She took a step, as if to cross the road.

'Film crew!' Louder this time, so she wouldn't come any closer. I needed to sit down, but I couldn't tell how far I was from the ground.

We both looked toward the light. Over the waves came a buzzing from the bay. I knew what that was, too.

'Speedboat,' I added as a matter of urgency.

She shrugged, like *what can you do, this crazy place*. I watched her shoulder rise and fall, her beautiful collarbones. My head was nodding slowly.

We looked at each other, the rustle in the palm trees, the film crew working, the speedboat on the waves.

I should have said more, but I could only speak in nouns. I had one more in me and then I needed to lie down.

'Night!'

Before she could reply, I scuttled back into the house and hid in my bed, staring at the ceiling, hot-cheeked. Hot in the sheets, my body reaching beyond its limits, an anemone waving in the water.

I WAS WATCHING THE SEA, high tide, low tide, pleading with the waves. The news said there were three hurricanes spinning across the ocean, part of a tropical storm. They were whipping up danger on south-facing beaches. In spite of such warnings, the ocean looked much the same.

My mother found me on a bench at the edge of our garden and sat, leaving plenty of room between us. A gust snatched at her hair. Mom started telling me about a cargo ship out in the middle of the Pacific that had been caught in a storm years before. Intermodal containers filled with rubber bath toys were batted off the deck by wind and rain. Tens of thousands of bright bobbing creatures spilled into the ocean: red beavers, green frogs, blue turtles and yellow ducks. Within the first year, my mother said, some of these 'Friendly Floatees' had washed up on the Alaskan coast, two thousand miles from where the accident occurred. She must have been sorry for what she'd said or how she'd said it and was offering me comfort, even if it was false hope. If a rubber duck could be found, so could my father. I remembered a news story I had read about human feet washing up on the shores of British Columbia. I didn't want to think of him in pieces.

'Rubber duckies. Thanks, Mom,' I said.

'It's ancient history,' she said and lit a cigarette.

Since she'd stopped working, instead of stories about ships and tariffs, she seemed more interested in women being ruined by divorce. Cautionary tales, like the one about the woman she had met in a parking structure near Rodeo who lived in her car. A divorcée who kept her hair in rollers, so she would always be ready for her day in court. In my mother's eyes, I saw my father being flung around the North Pacific Gyre.

The idea of selling the house had whipped up my castaway dreams again, my hope for his return. Maybe Dad had made it to San Nicolas Island. There, in the early nineteenth century, Aleuts hunting for sea otter decimated the local tribe. A rescue ship, the *Peor es Nada*, arrived to spirit the remainder of the tribe to safety on the mainland among the missions, but they left one behind. And maybe like this Nicoleña, who lived alone on the island for years, my father could also find a way to survive. The island was now a naval base, and that gave me hope. I imagined him being washed ashore on any one of the Channel Islands and being found. Maybe with amnesia. He might be in a hospital. In critical condition, in a coma, but alive. I was scanning the news. Making calls. Nothing.

Later that afternoon I drove to a small bay guarded by a group of locals who had surfed its break for generations. They'd know about this ocean, these currents, the stretch of coastline where it had happened. The waves were mushy, and only a few surfers were out. I wasn't carrying a surfboard, but still they shouted at me to go the fuck away as I came down the bluff. The one I recognized recognized me and hushed the others up. I found a spot on the rocky beach and watched the men in the water. The pack left the sea before dusk, and Krit and I hung back. He asked me about Ana and I told him we'd lost touch, which was true.

The last I'd heard from Ana was about a year after we graduated high school. I'd finally found a permanent place of my own and was still settling in, still getting in a rhythm of paying my own bills. It was good to hear a familiar voice, someone who knew me well. It was like old times until she started telling me about someone she was seeing, a classmate at university.

'What do your parents say?' I asked.

'They don't know. They wouldn't approve of him.'

'Oh.'

'We had sex,' she said.

'OK,' I said. I wondered if she thought of me as the person who took her virginity. I thought of her that way.

'I didn't come.'

This wasn't a friendly phone call. I could hear what she wanted, and I couldn't give it to her. I wasn't ready.

'I can't help you,' I said.

It was silent for a while, and then she said: 'I'm sorry.'

And that was it.

Krit built a fire in 'the fort,' a rock-and-cement shack with lean-tos thatched with palm fronds. The structure had gotten bigger since I'd last seen it. When we met him, he had been living between this beach and his van and did things for money that our parents never would've done. Ana had said she liked him because he was free.

I wanted Krit to tell me if my dad could've reached land, but instead I asked about the Catalina Channel. He lit up. Krit had swum it for the first time this year. He'd just missed his own deadline – his thirty-eighth birthday – but he completed the swim in record time. Had he always been so old, I wondered as he spoke. How young we were then. Her skin.

'I'm famous,' he said, catching my attention. 'People know me now. They got my picture up at Bizny's and everything.'

He mistook my expression and sweetly explained the secret of his success: it was all about luck meeting preparation. It had taken him longer than he expected to build up the endurance: races and open-water swims, day and night. Working his way up, mile by mile, fifteen, then twenty, then a few more for good measure because it was likely he wouldn't be swimming in a straight line. He'd gathered his support team and taken the boat to Catalina Island. Waited for the neap tide. The exhilaration of stepping into the ocean at midnight, body greased for heat. He swam toward the mainland with only the glow sticks on the escort vessels to guide him. One vessel trailed a rope on which his water bottles and mouthwash and energy gels were stuck with duct-tape and thick rubber bands, like cluttered kelp.

'You lose time if you have to swim up to the boat,' he said. Time was a matter of life or death. He said vertigo had set in at mile twelve. He started to freeze three miles out from the mainland. But: 'I rallied.'

The firelight danced on his powerful body. I wanted to be close to it. I wanted to know what it felt like to be in it – everything it contained and had accomplished, all it was capable of.

DEATH WAS A FEATURE along these cliffs. There were more or less permanent installations of flowers along the railings with their notices of slippery and unstable surfaces, the danger of death. By the time one bouquet of flowers, real or plastic, had been battered by the sun and wind, another would appear nearby, alongside faded Sacred Hearts and statuettes of the Virgin of Guadalupe. It wasn't only locals. People came in from all across the city to end their lives on our stretch of coast. It was what happened. Sometime in the nineties, the only other time I remember really feeling like we had neighbours, a group of concerned homeowners, including my mother, banded together to encourage the city to install warning signs along the cliffs. Clearly the railing wasn't enough, they argued. It didn't do much, but it was something: an action for the powerless to take. And when my father disappeared, the neighbours banded together again. When I came back from the bay that day, there was a casserole on our front doorstep, the first in a long while. Like the other notes, this one avoided his death. 'We're here if you need anything,' it said. I was grateful that someone was still thinking about our grief, even though there was nothing they could do. The casserole dish was still warm. I looked across the road and saw that there was a light on in the retired longshoreman's house.

I walked right up to the front door and rang the bell. I heard steps inside the house. A bolt, a chain, a simple lock.

It was her. Everything about her was clean and confident, take-me-as-I-am. She was a little older than I was, in her thirties, and looked like she had it all figured out, down to her bedhead hair. She was wearing sparkling silver platform shoes. And her denim shorts and cut-off T-shirt. Her body in those clothes in a house with all those daddies. I wondered how they looked at her. If she was wearing those shoes for them, the fantasy men I half expected to be lounging in her living room.

'Is this a bad time?' I caught myself staring at her shoes.

She bent her knee and grabbed the top of her foot, stretching her muscular thigh. I followed the line from hip to shoulder to eyes. She didn't seem to mind me looking.

'No.' She smiled.

'I'm sorry about yesterday,' I said. 'I was...'

'Totally baked.' She rolled her eyes. 'I know.'

I wished I hadn't brought the casserole. I didn't want her to think I was some casserole-making suburban stoner. I pulled the dish closer to me, and she snatched the note taped to the tin foil.

As she read it, the front door drifted open. No men to be seen, just an open-plan living area with panelled walls and the old dusty pink carpet.

'They keep leaving these for us,' I said.

She squinted at me. 'I'm Orly,' she said and reached out to shake my hand. I rearranged my grip on the casserole, but I freed the wrong hand and only managed to tickle her palm. I told her my name. She repeated it, then smirked and as she asked: 'Who's "they"?'

'The neighbourhood committee.' The very idea of it made me feel self-conscious. I didn't want her to think I was the kind of person involved with a neighbourhood committee either.

'What do "they" do?' The idea seemed to amuse her.

'Nothing really. It's just a bunch of, um, housewives freaking out about people ruining their view, but you don't have trees on your property, so...'

The silence between us. I hadn't noticed how close we were standing to each other. I felt myself sway.

'You smell like campfire,' she said.

I blushed.

'I was at the beach.'

'Here?'

I nodded, and regretted it immediately.

'I didn't know there was beach access here.'

'Technically it's trespassing, but there are some spots.'

'Will you show me?'

My head clouded with possibility: of being near her, that she was making plans with me already, and fear. When I said 'spots,' I was picturing the place my father disappeared. *No, I can't take you there,* I thought, while nodding yes.

She took the casserole from me. Her hands grazed mine. Orly lifted the foil from the dish and sniffed. The smell of tuna and onions rose between us. Something – potato chips, maybe – formed a jagged crust.

'Thank you for this.' She pinched the foil back in place. 'But one of my clients told me about a bar with a famous burger. I've kind of got my heart set on it tonight. You hungry?'

I knew what she was talking about, and I thought it was incredible that of all the places to eat around here, she wanted to go there. It was so late I'd been thinking I'd make a meal of hunger and let hunger put me to sleep, but instead I said, 'I'm starving.'

My parents weren't the kind of people who'd go to what they called 'the biker bar' by the park near the port. My interests, my friends, had taken me to different parts of town: large houses with no parents at home, busy beaches up and down the coast, and later, other large houses on other hills in a part of town that promised transcendence, but I hadn't been there. It was really more a café with a liquor licence on a street that was supposed to lead to a development of ocean-front homes that never got built. When they started laying the foundation nearly a century ago, the cliffs slid. Now what was left were broken concrete slabs bright with graffiti. There were lots of places to be alone, to build a fire and drink and hide. Once I'd seen a raccoon watching a cat looking at a blood moon while the buoys moaned.

Orly ordered the burger, a thin patty with American cheese. I liked how she ordered, no special requests, but she asked what made it famous and listened intently as the waitress explained. I ordered toast. Even though I was hungry, being here with her made me feel unable to eat. She had soda, I had a decaf coffee. She caught sight of something out the window and smiled. 'He'll only stay a minute,' she told me.

Then the screen door creaked as it swung open and a man with a skateboard tucked under his arm came in. The place was so small that this was all it took to make it feel crowded. The men at the bar turned to look at him and went back to watching the game. The man ordered a beer, and then sat next to Orly. There was nothing about him that I liked. He seemed to have a lot going on, a sort of agenda. Orly looked at him expectantly, but he just smiled and got comfortable. His name was Jordy.

Jordy looked me up and down as he said, 'Does anyone ever tell you you look like that actress…'

I shrugged.

He was so close I could smell the day on him, tar and stale tobacco. His skin was full of sun, hardened, and his gaze rested on me, like a drunk who uses his stagger as an excuse for being handsy. He wouldn't take his eyes off my breasts. Orly wasn't pleased. I could see her getting irritated as he made small talk. And yet, she didn't tell him to go away.

Eventually she said, 'Our food's getting cold,' to which he replied, 'Pshh.' Orly seemed to be reaching for him under the table. He held her gaze, smirking. Then he said,

'All right,' and put his hand in his pocket. Their hands met and she pulled away.

Jordy got up with a laboured sigh and picked up his plastic cup. It left a pool of condensation on the table. 'I guess I'll take this to go.' He lingered, looking at me. 'Nice to meet you, princess.'

From behind the bar, the waitress said, 'You can't take alcoholic beverages off the premises.'

Jordy shook his head, downed it in one, and left his cup on the windowsill. He let the screen door slam behind him.

'I'm sorry about that,' Orly whispered. 'He's the only dealer I've found who'll deliver here and get me what I want. Who cares about him. You're going to love his stuff.'

I tugged at my bra, making sure my breasts were contained. It was a gesture of habit, one I'm not sure I would have been aware of had Orly not commented on it.

'Those,' she said, gesturing at my breasts with a French fry, 'are gifts from the Goddess. They deserve to be admired, but men need to know their place.' She leaned in, and in a low voice she said, 'He does.' She waved at the youngest guy at the bar, who blushed when our eyes met.

Orly ate her burger in four bites, and I nibbled on the toast, just to have eaten something. The butter was margarine and the raspberry jam was little more than red sugar.

Orly could see I was nervous. She was being careful with me, careful to let me know that I could be quiet if I needed to be, but soon enough I was telling her about my father. She listened. Even if I hadn't been talking, I think she would have understood. When I felt the tears coming, I thought it might overwhelm her, so I changed the subject: 'Do you live alone?'

'I have a housemate,' she said. 'He's been setting up the place for me while I've been on the road, but it's been too much travel. If I have to spend one more hour with a suit in D.C....'

She giggled. 'I can't wait to set up shop at home, but it's still such a mess.'

'A few unpacked boxes aren't what I'd call a mess.'

'Sure, but it's not good enough. Lonnie's settling into something new, too, so I probably shouldn't be too hard on him.'

'Lonnie,' I said. 'I thought maybe he was your…'

'Boyfriend? Uh-uh,' she said softly and seemed far away when she added: 'But our relationship is the longest I've had with any man.'

'How long?'

'A decade, maybe.'

I didn't have any real friends I'd known that long.

'You have a lot of visitors,' I said. I was afraid I was giving away that I'd been keeping an eye on her house. She probably already thought I was weird. *Fuck it*, I thought.

She laughed. 'They're my clients.'

'What kind?'

Orly tilted her head and as though I should have already known, she said: 'I'm a dominatrix.'

My mind went blank. 'Oh,' I replied. 'Cool.' I did think it was cool, at least interesting, but it didn't seem like enough of a response. Maybe she thought I might judge her or cause trouble, but if so she wouldn't have trusted me with this information. I wanted her to think we had a lot in common, so I said: 'I work with my body, too.' I wasn't thinking about acting then, but art modelling, which felt like a lie. Having done something once doesn't really count as something you do. 'I work at the art centre as an art model. I thought all I'd be doing was getting paid for showing up and standing around however they wanted me to, but actually…' This occurred to me as I spoke: 'Being naked in front of all those people is sort of a relief. When the teacher and the sculptors are looking at me, there is no too thin or not thin enough, too weak or too old. No "They went in a different direction", "They loved your performance but they were looking for someone more conventionally attractive." They don't want any more than what I am giving them. I'm something to behold. It's a break from…' I nodded toward where Jordy had been sitting. 'I'm inviting them to look, and they can do what they like with the image.' I paused. I thought of Dr. Moradi's sculpture, that deformity he'd wrapped in damp rags to keep the clay soft for the next class. 'But it's not always pretty.'

Orly's silence and the way she was looking at me, calm and searching, made me think I'd struck a chord.

She said, 'No, it's not. It's not always pretty. It can be draining if you don't have a balance between give and take. To get there you have to have fun with it. Play. The hard part is most people don't know how to ask for what they want. They don't think they're allowed.'

Her words hung in the air. Orly had a way of making me feel seen and, in being seen, feel indecent. She could see how much I wanted, and how I was trying to push that want down.

As she was about to speak, her phone buzzed, and she excused herself to check a message. Her expression became mischievous as she engaged in a short text exchange. When she was done, she put the phone screen-down on the table. She said, laughing: 'The poor guy doesn't understand yet that sodomy won't resolve his self-loathing.'

My toast had gone cold. The phone buzzed again and she gave it a pat as if to calm it down.

Back at her house, she took out the eighth she'd bought from Jordy. We smoked on her sofa, side by side, looking out at the ocean. The night felt cold after the long hot day, and I pulled a throw blanket around me. When the smoke began to carve channels of silence between our words, I mumbled that I was happy we were neighbours, and I think she said, *It must be fate*. She smoothed the blanket over me, not touching me, but touching around me, tracing my shape, a touch I told myself to think nothing of, but which made me feel happy and queasy. I blamed it on Jordy's pot. It was a good strain, not like what I'd found in my closet. It made the world soft and quiet. Everything was murmur. Even her housemate leaving in the morning. I looked up from under my blanket on the sofa, still half-asleep, and saw the petite man, Lonnie, hurry out of the house in a white button-down shirt and jeans. *Housemate*, I thought and smiled. I closed my eyes again and listened to his car drive away, her house sounds, sensing the difference in the angles of the light at my house and here. As I drifted off again, I thought this is how it would feel like to be done grieving. It would no longer hurt to be awake, reconciling a reality in which Dad was alive and well with the one in which he was gone and I was looking for him in every other man. I ventured a thought in that direction, recoiled immediately, and focused instead on being in her home. Here, where it was soft and safe. Where men were put in their place. Where there was no dad or Daddy, just a housemate. And I could still be anyone with her.

Orly wouldn't let us leave for the beach until we'd found sunscreen for me. 'We don't want you to burn,' she said. It took her a few tries to find the cabinet with the towels, which were in the laundry room, and the sunscreen, which was in the guest bathroom. Every cabinet was meticulously organized. 'Sometimes he tries too hard,' Orly said of Lonnie. 'But when he sticks to doing what he's asked to do, he's perfect.' At first, sharing her gripes about her housemate felt like intimacy, but then it felt like a warning. How easily she could be displeased. How much I wanted to please her, and be praised after doing as I was told.

At the beach, I watched the ocean. Sailboats, surfers, swimmers, dolphin, no dolphin. Planes dragging banners through the sky. Our legs in the sun. I caught her looking as we talked, and was aware of how thick mine were. I wondered if she liked them or thought they were an indication of my lack of discipline. I told her, 'My dad said that if I ever needed to talk to him, he'd be here.'

'Have you tried talking to him?'

I shook my head and wiped the tears away with the back of my hand, but didn't realize it was sandy, and so suddenly I was holding open my eye while Orly poured bottled water into it. We couldn't stop giggling, and I saw Orly smile at someone as she kneeled over me, holding my head still against her toasted skin. Two men came over and Orly played with her wild hair and laughed at their simple jokes. She didn't tell them about her job. *If only they knew*, I thought. Orly told them her name was Coco, and I said mine was Lola. They wanted to get drinks with us, so we walked to a bar with greasy hamburgers, pool tables, and men who lived on boats. The man who was for me and I beat the other two at pool. It wasn't that kind of place, but Orly and I convinced the bartender to make us rum drinks adorned with candied cherries and slices of pineapple and dusty cocktail umbrellas he found behind the register. After sunset, she left with her man. When she hugged me goodbye, she whispered, 'Enjoy.' I wanted to tell her to drive away with me instead, but I watched her leave and watched mine go swimming. I could have told him about the hurricanes offshore, but what did it matter? I counted the seconds that he was underwater, trying not to think about what else was in there with him. One breath, two breaths, three and hold. Holding his breath so long it could have been his last. An organism, panicked, then limp. Pulled into an eddy.

We stayed on the beach long after dark. I hid my tears in the salt on his skin, and kissed them away again, kissed him as I would kiss her, loving his body as I would hers. The towels were wet and thick with sand when I was through with him. As I drove home, sore from the sun, I thought maybe one day Orly and I wouldn't need a proxy.

WEDNESDAY'S CLASS ROLLED around, and the artists tried to find me in their wet clay. I returned to my stillness, to my breath, radiating with thoughts of Orly, and found myself scaling the cliffs. Down on the shore, woman atop woman. The wind flipping through their salt-stiff pages; from their rustling rose my song.

Under Fumiko's watchful eye, the students scraped and pressed and shaped and cut in tune. I emerged, radiant in the logic of their architecture.

But no matter how hard Dr. Moradi tried, his sculpture stooped, lifeless, a sad tumble of clay. He was deaf to me.

After class, I saw him crying in the parking lot. Squatting against the stone wall of the room that housed the kiln. I pretended not to notice as I walked past.

'You fucked her up,' he said. And I froze.

The man was rumpled, seething. He stood, walked toward me. Stopped when he was already too near, poking my chest with his finger. I backed into a parked car. Red. Sporty. Familiar.

'I always knew you were trouble, but when I saw you, you two. I mean, look at you, look at what's become of you.'

You're here, too, I wanted to say, but there was no time. I tried to lunge away from the car, expecting him to move, but he stood his ground and pinned me to the driver-side door. I couldn't reach my car keys, what I'd always thought of as a weapon to hand, my arms flailing around his body, the long seconds, *go limp, go limp, go limp*, I told myself, but his body was holding me in place, and I let myself hang under his weight, his arm at my throat, and went a different kind of limp, the praying kind. I shut my eyes.

I thought he was going to hit me, but instead he grabbed me and slammed me against the car, winding me; my eyes opened in shock to see him red and wet, lips slick and trembling, his skin's oily sheen. Even his hairline seemed agitated. Tears mixed with his sweat. He hiccupped.

'She won't talk to me because of th-this,' he whispered, his free hand fumbling, groping, his sour breath on my cheek. I watched his face change, his short eyelashes stuck together, the deep frown lines. His pain. He had suffered her loss, too.

He looked at me with disgust. And then seemed to become aware of how our bodies were pressed together, a flicker of distress, what he might do next.

'You're a disease,' he said, and let me drop to the ground, pushing me out of the way with his foot. Maybe he could feel me wanting. Maybe this is what I get. The thoughts came unbidden. I didn't want them to belong to me.

He took the driveway too fast and at the wrong angle, first banging, then scraping the chassis. And drove off. Back to that house, I guess. A father who was not mine was driving home.

The parking lot was empty but for my car, and the sky was filled with stars. The breeze that rolled over those hills rolled on. The night was dark, and everything seemed as it should be, this pretty place with the salted air as it always was, no matter what happens between two people. I picked myself up off the asphalt, rubbed bits of gravel off the back of my thighs, in a parking lot in the part of town where once I had felt at home. The emptiness was large, the darkness a threat, yet the stars barely flickered. *Burn brighter, stars! Rain fire, stars!* Shaking. My keys. The door. The sound of the lock brought comfort. Curled up in the front seat. Trying to breathe. It was just me.

But then a door opened, light spilled out. I peered through my window, trying to keep out of sight. Fumiko was locking up the studio. It never occurred to me that she might take the bus. Or someone might be coming for her. Someone kind. Slender, slight Fumiko, who had not been slammed against a hard surface that night, who was not trying to remember how to breathe, *stop shaking*, Fumiko who might hold me, might tell me it will be OK, her clay-caked hands. If she discovered me, still here, stained, and asked if everything was OK, what would I say? What would she say when she saw me? I wanted to go back to where I belonged, to my own apartment, far away from here.

I turned the key, the machine smooth, efficient, fast. Sweet machine, dear machine. In the rear-view mirror, I saw her watching me go. She lifted a hand as if to wave, I raised mine as though everything were normal. I turned onto a residential street to avoid the red light.

The radio was playing an old but familiar song.

DO YOU REMEMBER that song? The one where the pop princess said she was not a girl and not yet a woman? The singer was stuck between the two states of being and thought she needed to take some time for herself, in order to become the woman she knew was inside her, waiting to emerge.

I liked that song, most every girl my age did. We loved the pop singer. Her bangin' body and rhinestone-coated jeans, flaunting a flat belly that could be made round. She was pretty, blond, and talented enough. A shining example of what a girl can achieve with hard work, tenacity, and luck. And she was all flaunt, no action: pure. It was crucial that we understood no matter how sexy her persona, she was still a virgin: not a girl, but not yet a woman.

The song reminded me of the power I had sensed as a preteen with budding breasts, before the invisible boundary lines were drawn between me and Ana. Only pretending not to notice the looks I was getting. It was strange to feel my body speaking when it was met by those gazes, without me ever opening my mouth. What was my body making of me? Was it a liability or an asset? I was unprepared. And yet I aspired to be a woman, not thinking of what that meant.

For Orly the song was a kind of anthem. The song was released the year she started working as a domme. Whenever she heard it, she felt a certain schadenfreude. As long as songs like this were hits, she said, she'd never go out of business. Hers was a healing practice, she said, and by creating a compassionate space, she was helping people to avoid unnecessary pain.

Orly had a theory. She laid it out the day we spent on the beach. It was her version of *Men Are From Mars* – an idea pieced together from stories of blood countesses, drawing down the moon, the is-to-be of a certain kind of sorcery, and doses of science, both soft and hard.

She thought, when she retired, if she retired, she might write a book. She imagined soliciting help from her clients, for who else could help her write it? A house full of men typing. I told her about the fantasy I'd had about all the daddies gathering at her home, like schools of fish. She listened and said, 'We can make that happen.' Her seriousness was intimidating. It couldn't be that easy.

Orly said her job was to help heal the rift between the sexes. It wasn't about flipping the script. Matriarchy wasn't the answer to our problems. We needed to see the value in the feminine and masculine, and then move beyond the binary, thinking of what unites us. To achieve this, she helped facilitate encounters with the feminine divine. She held the space for her clients and embodied the archetype that served the encounter best. But hers was a daunting task. The order of things was well-established. For women like us, the biggest fight was over control of our blood: how and when and why we bleed. Our blood was its own clockwork, but time was set by man.

With our first period, Orly explained, we stop being girls and the countdown to womanhood begins in earnest. When we bleed at the proper times and in the proper ways, we become women, complicit in reproducing an order imposed on us by men. Nothing we have achieved has rendered this order obsolete.

Lingering in the in-between – single, childless – is suspect and cause for speculation. Throughout the ages, medicine has explored the 'diseases of virgins,' women who've stayed too long in the in-between, not a girl and not yet a woman. For doctors feared what would happen to us if the blood had nowhere to go. Some thought it would flood our body, flood our lungs, make us yearn for death with a longing usually reserved for lovers, and we would wish to drown. Drowning. A bloodless death. A refusal to shed it.

The Ancient Greeks had a name for each of the blood spells necessary for a girl to become a woman. There was the *parthenos*, a girl who had begun to menstruate and was still in her father's care. The *nymphê*, a wife who has bled in her marriage bed. And last, *gynê*: woman, mature and reproductive, one who has known the lochial flow. The blood spells chart the path of a woman's life as moving from the care of one man to the next, never on her own.

I was reminded of the pop singer. She turned her back on the world that had shaped her and shaved her head. Some said she was sick, but she said she was feeling free. Maybe Dr. Moradi wasn't wrong. If there was a disease, I was not it. It was something I had contracted, born of the science that makes sense of sex through pathology, a patriarchal order that fails not only women, it fails us all. We weren't asking for a cure. We were finding ways to give ourselves the permission to be.

PIGGY

THE HOUSEMATE, LONNIE, who I would soon find out was called 'Piggy' for his love of each one of a woman's ten precious toes, kept hearing you could find anything on the internet. It was 1994. Chat rooms were thriving, connecting people in ways that hadn't been possible before. He wanted in on that, but for all the people clutching their pearls over the sexual overtures being made in these spaces, he was having no luck finding people of his kind. He had an idea of, but not a language for, what he meant when he said he was looking for sex. Tired of rejection and miscommunication, he started feigning outrage at the slightest impropriety. He draped himself in pearls just so he could clutch those strands in his trembling fists, trusting in the superstition that, to get what you want, you shouldn't say your wishes out loud. Even this failed to summon them, the people with whom he wanted to commune. The pervs, he concluded, borrowing a word. It made him feel uncomfortable and ashamed, but at least, he thought, there was somewhere he fit in.

Maybe a different keystroke would have changed his luck, but what was a person like him to do? A person without time, privacy, or space. The only computer he could use was at work, but he knew what he was doing online could get him fired. After a day of database administration, he'd stay late at his desk at the university, stealing only as many minutes as he could before he knew his wife would ask questions about the lag between the end of the work day and him trilling, 'Honey, I'm home.' Liz, who kept asking about the CDs offering minutes of free internet that had started turning up everywhere, stuck to pizza cartons and in cereal boxes, they even came with their mail-order flash-frozen steaks. He didn't want to bring his secret home, and the

CDs were taunting him, multiplying around him. He was afraid he would be exposed. He could always get another job, but what if his wife found out? He'd never find another woman to love him. This he believed to be true. To Liz the CDs were full of mystery and promise. She wondered: *Wouldn't it be fun, joining America Online?*

He stocked the freezer with pizza, bought different cereals, and cancelled their meat subscription. He bought his meat at the local butcher until a superstore shut the business down. But in the end, he could not enforce a distance. His secret would catch up with him at home.

UP THE ELEVATOR TO the rotating panorama bar. Tinted towers and boulevards, mountains rising from the smog. Waiting. The ice in the tumbler, the mountains outside. The ice, the view, the room. Ice, view, room. He was early.

He'd wanted to leave time to 'watch the city spin' (her words, not his) like they had on their first date, after a married friend he knew from church had insisted on setting him up with a 'lovely young lady,' which Liz was. He'd been unfair to her. And he needed her to know he was sorry. An apology to her was overdue. Still single after their divorce and now in middle age, he was ready for change.

Seven on the dot. There she was.

He still loved the way she moved.

She dropped into the club chair.

These were the words that broke years of silence:

'I couldn't find street parking.'

Liz looked out the window. He followed her line of vision. The bar had rotated, and now their view was of a cluster of highrises. In an office with a light on was a man hunched at his desk. In another window, a cleaner was at work.

'Are you watching the city spin?' he asked.

'Huh?' she replied.

Her whiskey arrived.

'I didn't think you'd ever want to see me again,' she said.

He could hear her rubbing her fingers together under the table – a nervous habit she'd always tried to break. The whiskey he'd been nursing was watery and tasted slick, like air conditioning.

She brought the glass to her nose and took a deep inhale.

'I shouldn't be here.'

'What do you mean?'

'Frank worries.'

She paused, waiting for him to understand. 'Once a cheater…?'

'You're kidding.'

She pretended not to hear him.

He remembered the guilt, the judgment. His physician said it was all in his head. He'd been able to get it up, but he couldn't follow through. Liz insisting it wasn't sex if he wasn't inside her. Humiliating him when he couldn't perform. It got worse when she felt her clock was ticking, even though he said she still had time. 'Men always think there's time,' she'd say, first in anger and later crying. Eventually he came undone.

Breathe. Do what you came here to do.

She sat up straighter in her chair. 'You need to know that I forgive you.'

'Right, Liz, that's exactly why – '

'God's plan for you was too big for our marriage to hold.'

From her wallet, she took a folded paper and put it on the table. 'I knew this wasn't a coincidence when you called. Look what I picked up on Sunday.'

A yellow flyer for conversion therapy, a hand-drawn illustration of the Sacred Heart, fire lapping at the thorns. He began to read – *Such were some of you; but you were washed* – then stopped. The woman wasn't his Lizzie.

Hand over his mouth, hiding a pained scoff.

'Bless you.'

Let her think it's a sneeze.

She squeezed his hand and said, 'See you soon.'

Screw being washed by the water of the word. He'd tried to get clean. Nothing could still his desire. Not work. Not abstinence. Not dedicating himself to the service of the greater good.

He didn't make it into the bathroom. The tears came by the pay phones. He sat down. He tried to pull himself together by taking in what was around. A carpeted hallway. A leatherette stool. Wood panels for privacy. The price of a phone call. The directory attached to the metal box with a metal cord. He read the instructions on the phone, trying to stem his thoughts and make himself stop crying.

Listen for the dial tone.

It's OK if you can't breathe.

Dial.

Focus on the breath. Observe it.

1 + Area Code + Number. Deposit Required Amount.

Take your time.

US Coin Only. Change Not Provided.

Breathe.

That's right.

Nice and easy.

You're fine just as you are.

He relaxed. Stood up, got ready to go back in and settle his tab.

And then the phone started ringing.

An incoming call.

THE RINGING.

He'd thrown away Liz's flyer but he couldn't get the ringing out of his head. Everywhere he looked: pay phones. The sight of them made him feel wild and focused. Alive.

There were months of searching and cold feet, searching and nerves. A mental map of phone booths across the city. He had to find the right one. Wherever he was temping, he made note. Wherever he ate, drank, ran errands, he made note. Commit nothing to paper. Save no documents. Leave no digital trail. He'd gone analogue since Human Resources called him in and that job went out the window. One day maybe, he'd find another nice university to work at. He'd always been good at data, the architecture of information. How to put things places where they'd stay until you needed them.

Pay phones at the French dip place where he took his lunch break when he was filling in for the clerk on maternity leave at Feinstein, Lavers & Witt. A man on the phone. Why wasn't he on his cell? Suspicious. He needed to find one that was private.

The phones at the Metro station where he could be anonymous in a crowd, but where it was uncomfortably empty between the trains and there was always someone lingering.

The phone bolted on the stone wall of Al's Bar, beyond the reach of the green neon and lights from the parking lot. A man leaning against it with his elbow on top, watching, watching, eye contact. Smile. A subtle gesture with the neck and eyes. *You got the wrong idea, buddy.* Head down, walk on.

The one on Sunset by the café with the outdoor patio. A glass box for people with nothing to hide. Wedged in a groove of the phone was a card with a busty lady begging him to call, but he had someone else in mind. He'd been dreaming of her since he was a child. Suddenly one day there she was, in a Superman comic. Proof that what he wanted did exist.

When Sapphire decides to be bad...she's very, very bad. Superman kisses Star Sapphire's pink boots in front of a gasping crowd. *Let the whole world see you've become my slave!* Superman rendered powerless by his female foe. An obedient slave. She gives him a 'practical task.' *Destroy the Galaxy Building and everyone in it! With that the whole world will know Superman is my obedient slave – for all time!* The things she makes him do. The moment Superman is set free. An inevitable release. It was all he could do to take the edge off – busy his hands with thoughts of Star Sapphire. When other boys talked about getting their peckers wet, he kept his mouth shut, thought of Star Sapphire and the humiliation he hoped she would make him endure.

TONIGHT'S THE NIGHT.

The black socks not the white ones, the dirt will show less though the lint will show more. But lint can be picked off, and dirt will make the fibres grimy.

The black socks are better for sneaking.

He'd always been good at sneaking. It was his second nature to hide.

But this sneaking is new.

This sneaking will lead to sneaking no more.

He hopes.

The backpack and the newspaper.

The pocket full of change.

The wallet, too. Never leave home without it. In case you get run over. In case they need to ID you.

This is too big for in here. Murphy bed and a bathroom in the hall. Paper thin walls. No place for this call. Don't want anyone listening.

Ear to the door. Listen for the chatty neighbours. Nope, no Nestor. No Fred. No Irma and her late-night callers who keep their eyes down and mouths shut until she lets them in. They've got it easy.

Unlock the door and scan the hallway. All clear.

Carry the squeaky sneakers in one hand and pull the door shut. Quietly, so no one will know. Remember to lock it.

Avoid the elevator.

Head for the stairs.

Or maybe the elevator.

No, no, the stairs.

Stop deliberating. Make a choice. Don't linger in the hallway.

Sit on the stairs in the stairwell.

Avoid the puddle under the pipe.

Check your soles. Already grey with dust and lint and that one red thread. If there is lint, there will be a red thread.

Filthy.

Pick the thread and lint from the socks, brush them off. Slip the sneakers on. Doesn't matter if they squeak on the floor in here. Tie them tight.

Down the emergency stairs, out the back, through the alley. Away from the pay-by-the-week hotel, through Skid Row to the edge of where's hip. Less than a mile, but a hot walk no matter how cool the night.

The Weekly in his backpack.

The shush-shush of denim.

Eyes on the street. Eyes from the street. *Nothing to see here.*

Pick up the pace. Hand in pocket, pocket full of quarters and dimes.

Jangle the change.

Jangle the coins until they begin to sing.

Tonight's the night.

There it was. Better than all the rest. Glass and steel. A door that shut, near a parking lot that closed at ten. No one around. Not a soul. But worth the risk.

Nervous fingers. Take a breath.

Unzip the backpack. Take the cloth from the packet and wipe the place down. The handset, the coin slot, the keypad. Lemon, metal.

Ready? Ready.

Take out the newspaper. Folded just so, for efficiency. Sun-crisp though it only dropped today. Had to be sure the ads were fresh. Current. Active.

Exact change. Wedge the phone between shoulder and ear. Dial tone. No one around. The coins go in the coin slot. Careful. Don't drop them. T-r-r-r-r. The machine is counting one by one. T-r. T-r. T-r. T-r. Until it is enough.

Type in her number. The clack and push of the keys.

Listen to it ring.

Glad to be contained. The pounding inside him. It can only grow as big as its cage.

It's ringing.

Oh God, it's ringing.

Ring.

Ring.

Ring.

Oh God.

'Hello.'

Oh God.

'Is someone there?'

Oh God.

Click.

The coins clatter inside the machine.

Change is not provided.

Phone on the cradle. Hand on the phone. Forehead on hand.

Oh God.

That one was just for practice.

THE SECOND TRY.

Blond, black roots, and a scowl. Cut-offs, old T-shirt. Nothing like her ad.

Hand on his arm, pulling him in. Take a good look outside, before the door shuts, the lock turns. 'You can put those there.'

Living room. He puts the roses on the coffee table between a bowl of seashells and the foil from a yogurt cup, yogurt-side-up, not quite licked clean. No vase. No 'thank you.'

'This way.'

A regular bedroom.

Something on the floor.

Fast-food wrapper.

Don't ask if the sheets are clean.

'Undress and lie down.'

Losing his balance as he takes off his right shoe. Pathetic.

Bed so soft he sinks in.

Smells clean enough. A little sandy.

Unsure of how to move.

Watch her move.

Feel excited.

This is it.

Leather cuffs around his wrists.

He wants to feel her skin.

He wants her to speak to him.

But instead she dives right in.

Riding crop.

Riding crop.

Riding crop.

Fuck.

Riding crop.

Try to catch her eye.

Riding crop.

Closing the eyes, thinking *Star Sapphire*. But all there is is riding crop riding crop.

Riding crop.

'Stop!'

Riding crop.

'Stop stop stop I'm serious stop.'

Silence.

His skin in flames.

'You said you wanted me to hurt you.'

TRY, TRY, AND TRY again, but he had to wait until he healed. Didn't want to give the next one the wrong idea.

The bean pole in the bathroom mirror.

He makes himself look.

Broken skin.

Ointment.

He reaches for his back, stretching his arm, reaching. Pushing his elbow with one hand so his finger can reach the wound.

So many hard-to-reach places. Imagine another pair of hands. Imagine coming home to them. Lover or friend.

Slick and antiseptic. The red marks shone.

To have brushed up against annihilation.

The sweet relief.

He hadn't wanted her to stop. He wanted her to stop. There was pain he craved, but her way had frightened him, unchecked and angry. He wasn't after a beating, not of that kind. His desire had frightened him. He had feared for his soul. What wanting this meant. If it was a sin. He feared he'd called the devil to himself, when what he was reaching for was divine. But who was he to say that God could be made of images from his own mind, and what did it mean when the image was shadow.

He felt sick inside.

The thing in his gut.

Stifled and writhing.

Begging for light to define it.

It wouldn't let him leave the flesh behind, no matter how he'd tried.

As the wounds healed, he felt better. The body mends itself. If body, then perhaps so mind. It knew how, and he followed its lead. He repeated his ritual.

He read the ads each week in *The Weekly*, collected coins, mustering the courage to return.

Dreaming of glass and steel.

The women behind the words.

Even when he wasn't outside, he had his hand in his pocket, his pocket full of change.

Jangling the coins in anticipation of the next time he'd be standing in a phone booth, feeling their weight in his hand. The coins. Cool at first, warming in his palm. The way they slip through the slot.

How they drop.

That thought alone, enough to make him hot.

Black bob, red lips, tight dress. Classy. She runs a red nail along the edges of the bills. Dollars he's saved. Singles and fives. A twenty.

The man in the kitchen.

A guy that size would make anyone feel safe.

Can't blame her.

A guy that size. Mighty as Superman. Deserving of what he desired.

Stilettos. Beige carpet.

Follow her into the next room. He notices himself hoping. Hoping she'll show him her feet. Hoping for red polish on the toes. Chipped on one maybe, but glossy. A foot stuck in stockings and leather all day. Damp. A slight callus. Feet that get used.

A room with blackout blinds, red walls.

'Welcome to my dungeon, worm.'

Worm. It's what they'd discussed.

'H-hello.'

'That's not how you address your queen.'

'I'm sorry.'

'Do you remember what we discussed on the phone? Do you remember who I am?'

'M-m-y qu-qu-queen.'

'Correct. Who do you serve?'

'You, Your Highness.'

'Good. That's how you'll address me. Do you understand?'

He nods.

'And what kind of queen am I?'

A collar around his neck. All of him that was expanding, now contained. Present.

'A size queen.' What else could he have said on the phone? She'd asked questions, made suggestions. 'Size queen' sounded good. It was the first time someone had really asked what he wanted.

'Damn right I am. Strip.'

Hesitation met with an unyielding gaze.

His shoes.

Her cold stare.

Socks.

'Look at your tiny feet. You've got feet like a girl.'

Eyes to the ground.

'You know what they say about small feet.'

'Yes, Your Highness.'

'What do they say?'

'Small feet, small…'

'Small?'

'Small penis.'

'I can't hear you. From the top.'

'Small feet, small penis!' Voice unusually loud. But he likes the way it feels. Doing as he's told.

'Good boy.'

Yes.

She takes him by the chin and makes him look at her.

'Do you think you're fit to serve this queen?'

'No, Your Highness.'

'And yet you came.'

Cold eyes.

He shudders.

She notices. Giggles.

Shirt off.

'You *are* a wimp.'

Then pants.

'Look at those skinny legs.'

Circling him. Close enough to feel her heat.

'Do you really think I'm looking forward to seeing that little willy of yours, worm? That cocktail weenie. That limp dick. Your tiny prick. That useless speck between your legs.'

All the men she must have seen. Maybe his *was* a speck compared to them.

'No, Your Highness.'

She snaps the elastic of his underwear.

He feels the fear. Remembers she'd asked about limits. He said no beating. It was all he could say until he figured out what kind of pain he wanted. Trust her. Trust her to have listened. Breathe.

'Well, you're wrong, pinkie dick. I'm looking forward to having a chuckle.' Softer now: 'On your knees.'

Towering over him. Short dress. A glimpse of red lace panties. Fragrant. Yes.

Shoe nudging cock. Her laughter.

'All my girlfriends are going to laugh so hard when I tell them what a little man you are. They're going to laugh so hard they're gonna wet their white cotton panties.'

Wet panties. Yes. Wet white cotton panties. All the women. Thick ones with large breasts that jiggle when they laugh. Thin ones who titter. Uninterested blonds who barely crack a smile. And this one, his raven-haired queen laughing at him. Pointing and laughing until he's nothing. Yes. Nothing. Because he's not worth her attention. And she won't let him forget it. She has him, and won't let him go until she's good and ready.

'Oh you like that, do you? You like thinking about all those women. Laughing at your dicklet? You're a sissy with an itty-bitty clitty.'

Yes.

'Think of all the women who'd be let down by that itty-bitty clitty. All those women who expected a real man, but instead they got you. A sissy bitch.'

All of them. Every single one.

He sullies the tip of her stiletto. He didn't mean to but he likes it so much he's leaking.

'Pathetic. You should be holding that in until I tell you to come. Clean it up…'

'No, with your tongue.'

'Good. No one wants to see that from you…Or that.'

She points at his erection, straining for her. And all her friends. Yes. The size queens hungry for more. No less than nine inches will do. Disappointed by his dicklet. His itty-bitty clitty. The look on their faces, the blonds. The thin ones. The thick ones. The first and only other one who'd seen his cock straining. Her face.

Hers.

The chills.

Her.

Lizzie, disappointed. Again and again. The man he couldn't be.

The tears come. They don't stop.

'There, there.'

And then she waits.

Impatiently.

Waiting.

'You've been adequately entertaining, but if you keep on like this – '

Wet eyes, tears on the carpet. He senses her disgust.

They're done.

She's not the one. She's a woman, and he's a problem. A naked stranger curled up on the carpet. Deaf to her demands. The party guest overstaying his welcome. Immovable and aware. Aware of each hair on his skin. His sex dangling. His saggy tits. A little sissy bitch. Not enough hands to cover up.

Stop thinking about your nipples. Breathe. This is your body. This is where you are right now. Be grateful you have your body to carry you out of here.

Underwear first, then shirt. Pants socks shoes.

Step by step. In silence. Past the man in the kitchen who watches him walk out and locks the door behind him.

And there he is: in the hallway of an apartment complex all alone. Where to go? Where to take these feelings? He's been punished enough. He thought she was going to care. He pounds her door, a single solid thud. Bam, he doesn't want to be left out. Bam, he checks his watch, yes this is still his hour. And he has needs that she has not met. Bam. This wasn't what he was paying for. But no one answers. He presses his ear to the door; nothing. There will be no refund. No customer service complaint. No police report. No business here. He's trespassing.

Alone in someone else's hallway.

Surrounded by locked doors.

Inside him, the thing is pounding.

Be still, he wishes.

Be still.

ANOTHER ROUND.

'On me.'

The voice pulled him out of darkness, just enough so he could see.

'You don't have to do that.'

'I take care of the good ones,' Makena said. She poured herself one, too, and they drank. The whiskey and the kindness stilled the quaking inside, but it moved to his eyes again. He was tired and sore from crying.

'I'm one of the good ones, huh?'

'You always have cash. You never ask the girls if they like to floss when they suck. And you never wear shorts.'

'Hah,' he said. It was as close to laughing as he could get.

Makena took out a fresh bowl of nuts just for him, ones that hadn't been sitting out on the bar for god knows how long. She stood there, looking at him looking at his glass, and when he didn't look up she went back to reading her newspaper. He couldn't bear a woman's kindness right now, their sweet attention was not enough. This kind of attention he had no shortage of. Women liked him. He liked that they liked being friends, even though he could tell when knowing about his kink meant they stopped thinking of him as sexual. He knew well enough by now that there was no point pursuing something where it wasn't wanted. But today, he wanted something to go his way, one smooth transaction. That's it. And it was going to be easy, dammit. All he had to do was ask.

Late afternoon. The place was dead. The girls were keeping themselves occupied. He had enough cash. An advance on next month's fun money; he'd just about be able to make rent if he stuck to oatmeal and noodles. He had a good shot. And maybe an hour tops to make it happen, about an hour before the after-work crowd rolled in. Men who blew off steam. Men who had no qualms about commanding erotic attention, who felt entitled to it. Men who weren't given to worship, men who didn't need to knock to be let in.

He took his drink to the front row by the stage in the corner. Cool air streamed from the ceiling vents. He had to switch seats a few times before he found the right spot. Not too hot, not too cold. At just the right angle so he didn't have to see his own reflection in the mirrored wall or the man slumping against the stage and who seemed to be sleeping. No competition.

Roxie was running her routine like a rehearsal. Slow and acrobatic. She was rusty. Not quite as strong. Rumour had it a regular bought her those breasts, and she'd holed up in his place on Stone Canyon while recovering. Another girl said she'd seen Roxie in the parking lot of a strip mall in the Valley loaded up with bags, accompanied by someone who was definitely not Mr. Stone Canyon. It didn't matter, everyone said she liked playing wifey for men who had enough cash to hold her attention, and the girls liked to talk. He couldn't afford to be one of those guys. She cottoned on to that real quick. By ignoring him, she had grown inside his mind into something extraordinary. He ascribed intent to each time she failed to meet his eye. Each time she brushed past him. Her sugary perfume. It was all a tease. A tease. And on a dead day like this, at a time like this, maybe she could be the one. He was ready for it.

He settled in and followed the flick of her wrist, the curve of her spine. The shapes she made, the music flowing up through her high heels, twining itself around her thighs. Thrust and pulse, all woman. She did not need his eyes, but she invited them to rest on her. Some days this was enough. Being allowed to look, to partake in her beauty. Some days this was all it took for him to feel human, worthy of attention and love.

Roxie swung her feet up and wrapped her ankles around the pole. Her top hand had a twisted grip. Slowly, she piked her legs and steady steady steady stretched out into an X, but after the sha-boogie-bop she began to shake. Veins rippling. Hips and legs twisting to the ground, she landed with control. He whooped.

She flipped her hair and looked over her shoulder, holding his gaze as she walked away from him. As if she knew he had been waiting, as if she had been waiting for this, too. A different yearning began to rise. To see her smile. To be the cause of her smile.

He looked at the money in his wallet. Most of the dollar bills had gone fuzzy with age. One still had a newly minted sheen. Perfect.

Roxie walked past him in her clear platforms. He watched those shoes fly into the air as her legs twisted up and around the pole, spreading into something that made him think of Cupid. She grabbed the stiletto heel. He wanted it in his mouth. She slid to the floor and clapped her shoes together. The smack. He wanted her to clap them again and again and again.

His hands worked quickly, folding the crisp dollar bill this way and that, tucking it here, pulling it out there. A few adjustments. Yep, almost. Almost. OK. Fan it out and voila. A butterfly. He was known for his origami. The ladies liked it. They liked being surprised.

He held up his butterfly and Roxie made him wait before she came over. She offered him the elastic of her silver booty shorts. He shook his head 'no.' She offered him her cleavage. No. The bikini strap lying across her clavicle. No. The nape of her neck where the halter was fastened, lifting up her hair, a glance over the shoulder. Her muscular back. No. She ground down, writhed in front of him, and when her feet were within reach, he sat up in his chair. All he could hear was bass. A clear plastic strap fogged with sweat held her foot in place and made the skin glassy. He slid the abdomen of the butterfly between her first and second toes. It was tight in there.

Those majestic legs, towering, putting him in his place, where things were clear and safe.

This is it. He could feel it. He said the words to himself and said them again. So, the thing had a language, he marvelled as he spoke, each word a bright pearl. The words seemed so simple now. How had it taken him so long to find them? Looking up at her from the foot of the stage, he waited for his yes.

But it didn't come.

Roxie said: 'No, sweetie, no. That's not what I'm here for,' and laughed as if it were nothing.

He stood up fast. Salt in his eyes. Chest tight. An inner revolt. Everything around him reeling. Bar, woman, lights. The sick-sweet smell of old beer. The chair he'd missed, so he was crouched on the floor. Head to knee. The thing inside him squirming, he knew its language now, and it demanded to be heard. And the pearls, they kept rising. Clustering in place of air. Retch. Clenched teeth. Keep it in. Choke it back down.

Just when he didn't think he could hold it in anymore, she appeared.

A pair of hands, cupped.

A voice that said:

'Go ahead. Spill.'

And he did. He let everything rising roll out, each perfect pearl, they poured into her palms. No matter how many there were, Orly could hold them.

THE LOVERS

I DROVE AWAY FROM the art centre, as if I could leave it all behind. I drove and drove. So many miles. I drove up the 110. I texted the musician; he told me to come on over. I took the exit for the 405.

The further away from the peninsula I was, the better I felt. Hurtling along the city shallows, night in neon, the twinkling towers, I exited and took the street that led through the gates and wound up the hills, past a pink hotel hidden by palm trees where the musician kept saying he wanted to take me to try the lavender crème brûlée but never did. It was the thought that counted to him; he was thoughtless, but I didn't mind. Counting the streets past the hotel. I missed the turn almost every time. Counting. I could never remember the street name. Miravista. Loma Linda. Altamira. But I found it. A narrow street with smaller houses, modest family homes, wood siding and shingles, houses left over from a time when wealth meant something else, but my lover was further on. You'd miss it if you didn't know it was there. Mistake it for a fire road. The long driveway unfurled, a cat's tongue along a wall holding the land in place. Freshly waxed cars, curves and chrome in the moonlight. Los Angeles cascaded from the edge, a pitch-black shore, a sea of lights, the entire city, stretching out and out, bright, bright and far. Where I was from was only a shadow interrupting the horizon line. He had left the door open for me. I took off my shoes in the entryway and sank into the thick white carpet.

The air in his room was stale. He never opened the window, and every surface was heavy with items displaced from a house he no longer had in the 'arty' part of town he still called home – vintage vases, velvet paintings, piles of beads and fabric swatches.

Since we'd left the basement bar where we first met last spring, he'd been saying that he was only staying at his parents' house for a little while. We'd danced until they turned on the lights, and as we walked through the alley to his four-wheel drive, he made it clear he wasn't looking for anything serious. *Perfect*, I said. *Neither am I.*

He didn't look up when I walked in. He lay on the bed, concentrating on the glow of his laptop. Something, maybe a bat, tripped the security light outside his window and he winced.

He stopped typing and took off his headphones. 'I've been working with a new drummer. He toured with Iggy Pop. Listen.'

I was happy to be here with him, where I knew how to be and no one else knew where I was. Where men like Moradi would never find me.

I put on his headphones.

'The hook. It's like…' I pumped my fists, arms close to my chest, the music reminded me of that new song on the radio. The one everyone knew the moves to. I found the footwork, the swish of my hips. I curled my hands into claws. '…this song, you know? But with piano instead of a synth,' I said, swinging my claw-hands to the left and right.

He glared at me and turned off the music.

'What?'

'She stole my hook.'

I didn't know who he was talking about.

'Yeah. We used to play together. On that piano.' He pointed toward his parents' living room, which seemed to be forever expecting company. 'And this.' With a sweeping gesture that took in his entire body. 'Latex outfits. The "Sirocco Rococo" look. That's me. Those are my words.' He turned his hands into claws and shook his head. I hadn't ever bothered googling him, so I only knew what he told me and that no one I knew had heard of him or his band.

He shut his laptop and rubbed his slim face. He groaned into his hands and jumped to his feet. 'But fuck it.' He paced around the room, managing not to trip on the clothing and trinkets scattered on the mauve carpet.

I leaned against a sliver of bare wall and listened.

'My attorney says I have a case, but this isn't about winning the battle. She may have – ' He did the claws again. 'But she doesn't have this.' He pointed to his head. 'I've got a new drummer. I'm talking with an investor about my clothing line. I'm gonna blow up.'

He grabbed me by the waist. 'You see my world, Echo.' He pressed his palms together, still, finally. 'I'm going bring beauty to the people. I'm going to show them what the internet is for.' He stared into my eyes. His vision of the future was all that ever really got him hard. It was baroque. He needed to picture it, and then he needed a witness. He smiled, baring his goofy teeth. They never failed to charm me.

'I want you,' he said.

He fell to his knees and pushed up my T-shirt dress. His tongue, his fingers slipped in. He threw me on the bed. 'I've been taking these steroids for my allergies,' he said. 'I did weights last week and *boom*.'

We looked at his arms. They did look bigger. How hard he fought to be fey, his body conspiring against him, building muscle and bulk as soon he was anything but idle, pronouncing itself a man, masculine, male, in spite of his objections. He put my hand on his biceps.

'You feel that? I gotta watch what I eat or I won't fit into my vortex suit.'

He lubed me up in silence. He took his time, as one should. Relaxing the muscle, as one should. I focused on the sweet stretch and ache and let go, emptied my head, and he fucked me with devotion, stroking my hair and mumbling. I kept my body angled so he wouldn't put his weight on my tender side, the reminder of that pain. I think I was still in shock, carrying on as though everything were normal. When we found our rhythm, I reached between my legs. He finished too quickly for me to come, and I wasn't prepared for the disappointment, but it didn't last long because he didn't stop. He made a show of flipping me over with his big new muscles, which we both found funny. I remembered why I kept coming back. His touch was curious and sincere, intuitive in ways his narrative self was not.

He started to work his fingers inside me. One, two, three. The sensation was not of hand and cunt, but of diving in the dark. Unbearable, wonderful tension. Four, five. Until he could make a fist. Large and slippery inside. I ached, and he put his mouth to me and rested one hand on my chest. Tender. The waves of pleasure were warm swells at first. My mind let go and, through my half-shut eyes, his hand became Orly's. It was a different kind of ache, and I didn't fight it. I wanted to know where it would go, and there was no safer place to dream than here. As my heart sped up, racing, racing like when it had last raced, racing against Dr. Moradi's forearm, it whipped up a storm.

The musician read this as pleasure. In a way it was. I was also remembering her. He ground into me, moved his tongue faster. My heart, my breath, took me back to the panic, the mouth and the fist. Alongside my orgasm, sorrow and fear coursed through me. Slammed me against a car. Left. Everyone always leaving. Leaving me alone. I nudged him away from me, like I did when even the softest touch was too much.

He pulled his hand slowly out from me and flexed his arm. He grinned at his biceps, his hair in ropes, and he stretched out his hand for me to see and said, 'Everyone needs to be fucked like a lesbian once in a while.' Only then did he notice I was crying.

'Are you OK? Was it OK to do that?' He wiped the tears from my face with his dry hand and cradled my head. 'Babe, it's OK.'

I nodded and I let him pull me into his arms and told him that there was something with my heart. Its beating had felt more like danger than desire…it wanted out. I sobbed into his chest, comforted by his green scent, the way his hair tangled in my hands when I grabbed at his back. 'I just want you to hold me,' I said, thinking of how rested I felt waking up on Orly's sofa. Falling asleep without waves crashing inside my skull. I breathed him in until my breath was even again.

'You can always turn to me. I got you,' he said, wrapping his arms around me.

I didn't want to talk, so I kept quiet.

'You can't do this for as long as we have…as intensely as we have…' He was squeezing me too tight. '…And not start feeling things.'

I wrung myself out of his grip. 'That's not what we agreed,' I said.

He shook his head at me, like I was a child mispronouncing 'spaghetti.'

'You don't want to be tied down right now. I get it. I can be patient for you. You've been AWOL for weeks, and I didn't even text you. That has to count for something. And, I mean, I wasn't reading you my lyrics for nothing, right? I don't just tell people my plans.'

His grand plans involved big names and expensive people like attorneys, but never seemed to be moving forward because he was still at his parents'. But my silence had apparently been speaking volumes to him. I had liked our clean deal. I had liked that everything was on his terms. That he never offered to come to my place, that he only ever talked about us going out and then showed me all the places he'd had his picture taken. This was good. I could relax into our time together by letting him lead and letting our bodies talk, our wordless intimacy. We couldn't start talking now. This was a person who didn't know I no longer had a dad. It would have been reasonable to tell him, but maybe I'd wanted to come here because I thought of this space as autonomous, a fantasy, not a place where I could be visited by death. I thought of the calipers and dug my nails into my palms to keep the tears at bay. I said: 'I didn't even notice you hadn't texted.'

With that, he took his hands off me. 'You're un-fucking-believable,' he said. He adjusted his pillows, pulled the duvet over himself. He grabbed his computer, illuminating his bed with its glow. I hadn't meant to be so cruel. I wanted to apologize, but before I had a chance, he said, 'You can let yourself out.'

I DIDN'T KNOW WHAT I was doing. I hadn't thought it through. As I took my usual route from his house to my apartment, it settled in. The last time I'd driven down these streets, my dad had been alive and well. And the idea of my apartment frightened me. I hadn't been back there. It would reek of 'before,' of a time when I knew that, if things went wrong, he'd be there to protect me. Dad was a safety net. I could still be a child with him. I could always say that the life I was living was just pretend.

The light in the carport was flickering. When I shut off the engine, I locked the doors and leaned back in my seat, staring out the windshield at the stucco wall and listening to the cars pass by on the road behind me. I held on to the feeling of being on my way somewhere, travelling with purpose even if travelling was the purpose. When I was in transit, I didn't need to do anything but focus on the road, the car, the mirrors, brakes, and turn signals, how and when traffic slowed. The other lives on the road.

My apartment would be as I left it, but everything had changed. Maybe I should leave that space uncontaminated and drive back to my mother's, where these emotions already had a home. But this would mean another forty minutes in the car, forty minutes hurtling at top speed, catching shadows out of the corner of my eye. I pictured the geometry of the freeway, how light skates across its shapes in the dark. Wheels vibrating on tined concrete, racing toward a vanishing point. It wasn't human. I couldn't do it without falling apart. Maybe, I thought, I could sleep right here.

I ran my hands over the edges of the instrument panels, the assist grip and the puffy fabric around the vanity mirror, feeling its plastics and leathers and rubbers, all the bits drivers shouldn't touch while driving. I let the windows fog. I drifted off but jumped when something dropped onto my roof from the jacaranda growing on the sidewalk. It took a minute for the world to stop swimming, for me to make sense of the shadow and light. I thought about the noise of the outdoor coin-operated washing machines at the back of the building being used at night. The things I'd found discarded there.

I hurried through the front gate, keys in hand. I unlocked my front door. My studio apartment was airless and hot, a shoebox space that let all the noise in. The stale old-carpet smell. The venetian blinds were closed, the curtains I'd hung were drawn. I got into bed without turning the lights on. My sheets did not yet smell like sorrow. I feel asleep inside that dream.

When I woke, there was seaweed stuck in the outboard motor, pillow wet, tangled sheets. I kicked myself free. I pushed my face into my pillow like I wanted to press my nose into the groove of Orly's collarbone, imagining she would let me, and all I had to do was ask. I cupped my hands between my legs, and then my phone rang. I let it. They left a message.

I only realized what I'd been hoping to hear when I heard who it was on the other end. Then the dread set in, the pain of habits breaking, the sound of life skipping to the next track.

'Surprise, surprise,' my mother said. A fog had rolled in over her vowels. I wondered how long she'd been keeping herself hazy. If I had driven her to it, like him, to her cigarettes. 'You left.'

The wash of guilt left me sticky with resentment. How dare she. I couldn't get angry; she was too good at turning my anger around, making me out to be the one who needed fixing. I swallowed it down.

I heard the flick of a lighter. The storm when she exhaled. In a sing-song voice, she said: 'I'm smoking.' I listened to her take another drag. 'No more hiding it from your *fahder*.'

I couldn't remember the last time her tongue had stumbled. I had all but forgotten it could. *Fahder*. Her pronunciation made me nostalgic – the easy plenty contained in the word 'home.' I reached for the feeling, eager to touch it, but it was beyond my grasp and then gone.

'He liked to play high and mighty but he was worse than me! He said that if I thought of you, it would make me quit. But look at us now.' She cackled.

My hand was sweating against the phone. I wedged it between my ear and shoulder and wiped my palm on the sheet. It was just like her to pry open my heart only to shiv me through the crack.

English was my mother's third language, after German – her family's tongue – and the Dutch she learned in Rotterdam. Three, that is, if you're not counting the snatches of Italian she still remembered from the summer boyfriend she had at sixteen. Piero. I liked listening to her say his name, the warm rumble of her *r*'s, a sound I could never quite master. I liked hearing their story, even with the way she pressed her past into tokens.

Piero was a student from Genoa working on the ferry to Capri for the summer, she'd say. (The implication: *Only industrious men are worthy of your attention*.) They held hands and never kissed. (*Chastity is a thrill in itself. There is power in restraint*.) And were discreetly escorted by her father, who walked ahead of them on the esplanade, generously offering them the privacy needed for romance to bloom. (*I was raised with an easy love. Any difficulty between us is not my fault*.) Her father was a saint, and it was really so sad I'd never had a chance to know my grandfather before he died. (*There's something missing that you can't have*.)

At the end of the summer, she left with only the memory of Piero. They didn't exchange addresses. They made no prom- ises to keep in touch. This detail scandalized me; the idea that love could be temporary. To which she'd respond: 'Only death is eternal.'

Then she'd say that's how Vesuvio got his name. Vesuvio then Vivo then Herr Vampirzahn and Mr. Bitey then Vee for short. Vee was the tomcat she brought with her from Rotterdam. He was offish with everyone but her and painfully effective at catching birds. She doted on the cat, making special trips to a Croatian butcher near the harbour to buy offal, railing against 'America' for trying to gloss over the role death played in the omnivore's diet; she called the gutless grocery store chickens in Styrofoam trays wrapped in plastic foil 'perverse.' I thought of Vee as Piero incarnate, my orange summer love stalking past my window, sunning himself in our backyard. I learned to be patient, to wait for his affection, grateful for whatever cool caress he offered in passing.

Vee was the only witness to a life that my mother referred to as 'real.' Whatever romance my parents' story had was filed to a point with the statements beginning with 'your fahder.' My father expected us to be at his beck and call, didn't know how to take vacation, loved his work more than he loved us, always wanted to go running when it was time for family dinner. My father treated us like things to be arranged in his life, like the furniture in our house. She complained as she drove me around, carting me along on her errands, to my activities; I was her captive audience.

One day a new complaint appeared, sun on polished steel. It was about a year after they'd gotten back together after the separation. It was a day like any other. My mother picked me up from school, chest red and blotchy. A sign of upset I had learned to recognize, even when she insisted it was allergies. Like the tears that escaped her eyes. One, two drops rolling down her proud cheeks as she pretended to yawn. I was hoping to talk to her about the fifth-grade science fair, but she began to rant.

A rant I had heard before. About her desire to go back home – Munich or anywhere else she had lived before here, she didn't care – to claim the life she wanted to have, close to family on the continent. The continent: where life would be better for me and for her. Where I could have a real childhood. She always spoke in terms of 'we' as though her life were my own. But I only knew her Europe from holidays – whistle-stop tours of family and friends from Lake Constance to the Baltic – but my life was here. Incomplete as she insisted it was.

On this particular day she tacked on something else: a rant about the business my father had started and how if he had never struck out on his own, the shipping company they had worked for could have transferred him anywhere but here. But no. 'Your fahder' made sure that our lives were in arrest. She concluded: *American men are excellent salesmen, schatz. Like your fahder. Watch out or you'll get stuck with something you can't return.*

It was clear that the life she had dreamed of had never included frozen orange juice concentrate and so many hours spent finding parking. Perhaps her disappointment was her way of reminding herself that the woman she understood herself to be was not gone, just dormant, and could rise again. We had this in common: I think she was trying to make sense of herself here.

Instead of going home, we drove to her first elocution class. The tutor's office was on the second floor of a shopping mall covered in Spanish tile, meant to look like the Old World. You could allow yourself to believe you were on a narrow street some-where in Andalusia. It was one of her favourite places to go. She forgave 'America' its tolerance for artifice when the aesthetic suited her. Listening to the burble of the fountain in the courtyard, I plotted my science project in the tutor's waiting room, making lists of things I was curious about: how long it would take for the sea air to devour the wreck of a container ship, the husk of which was corroding on a nearby shore, if there really were shrimp in the tap water in other parts of Los Angeles, what would happen to our lungs if the teachers didn't make us stay in our classrooms during a smog alert. I had my own mysteries to solve.

Her first elocution lesson was scheduled on a day when I would have otherwise had a free afternoon – no tutor, no team sports, no horseback riding. She wanted to show me I wasn't the centre of her world. She had a life too, and sometimes her life required me to wait, dinner to be served late and not be home-made. ('Mom' was a gift, not a given.)

Before she started working with the voice coach, she did all the things the other moms I knew did, but she made clear it was a nightmare made bearable only because of me. She had always wanted to be a mother, she said. But she could be so busy moth-ering that being her daughter felt incidental. I could have been anyone, but she'd be this mother no matter what.

Her accent faded quickly. She said her tutor said she had a musical ear. But as the accent faded, so did she. I never thought I'd miss my embarrassment over her not wearing a bra and her conviction that there was nothing indecent about it. I never thought it would make me sad to watch her transition from brunette to blond, to give up a tailored seasonal wardrobe for jeans and jersey knits. She started arriving early enough for after-school pick-up to join the other mothers who gathered on the steps in their tennis whites to talk about their tennis instructors, their tennis bracelets glinting on their wrists. By the time I was a pre-teen she had become a person who fussed over surfaces: kitchen countertops, the cleanliness of floors, me. She was forever smoothing the flyaway hair at my temples, tugging at the hem of my uniform skirt. My mother didn't reminisce about Europe anymore, in general or in part. And whenever I asked about Piero, she'd change the subject. My father seemed relieved. He touched her more often, hugging her from behind and saying things like 'Nice to see you're in good spirits.' When she knew he couldn't see, she'd let her face fall.

It was during this time that they decided to stop smoking. My father went on one of his health kicks – lean proteins, low-fat yogurt, and smoothies none of us liked. Hints of pine and ash no longer accompanied their wish for me to sleep well. But she still smoked when they argued. Sometimes she stayed late on the balcony, and I'd sneak upstairs and sit with her. She'd say the ocean looked like quicksilver from here, and it made her feel like she was stuck at the end of the world. The house they'd built wasn't really for them, but what would they have left if they tore it down?

During their fights, I would hear my mother say, in her new crisp diction: 'Look at me. I'm killing myself for you.' To which he'd reply: 'I didn't ask you to.' I wondered how a marriage could turn into such a terrible misunderstanding. It inevitably came back to the smoking: the virtue of his having quit, and her ruinous decision to endure.

Look at us now.

I tried to put my mother's phone call out of my mind. I tried to put next week's art class out of my mind and focus on my apart-ment, my space, the life I had chosen. I ignored Fumiko's call when Wednesday night rolled around and I deleted her voicemail without listening to it, even though I needed the money from the job. The thought of honouring any commitments made my arms weak. I didn't want to hear what a disappointment I was. I tried to stop time. I stuffed the minutes with the nothing-fluff of days: rummaging through cupboards and drawers, writing emails to my old agent that I didn't send, and one to his assistant, Van, which I did, reading through *Backstage West*, Craigslist, listening to daytime radio. Feeling triumphant that it was not yet three and I could still...dejected when the clock struck four because time had slipped my grip and run away from me. I would stare into the night, sure the force of my gaze would keep the sun from rising.

VAN WAS IN SUIT AND TIE, parked out in front of my apartment building. He was blocking in the other cars as he opened the passenger door for me.

'Meet my new baby. Check out her headroom,' he said as I buckled myself into his 1986 911 Turbo, words he relished saying. With good reason. It was a beautiful car, down to the way the rear tires filled out the fenders. 'Leaving Jake was the best decision I ever made.'

Van smiled. He had new teeth, large, impossibly white and straight. I smiled back, displaying mine. I was born with perfect teeth. Casting agents liked them. I rarely left a call without being told they were pretty or asked to smile one more time. I think they wanted to know if I could do 'sunny.' People here seem ill at ease if you can't. I needed to smile to get there. My bone structure was Old World. A face for witches, exiles, scullery maids, the down-and-out. My mother's. I looked similar enough to Lola LaForce that people had to look twice, but she had what I did not: a generous mouth. It made her immediately likable. Sunny. It was why she'd gotten all the good roles both of us had been sent out for, and her career had taken off whereas mine had floundered. I used to stand in front of my mirror, hooking my pinkies into the corners of my mouth and pulling it wide, counting how many teeth you could see then compared to when I simply smiled. When Lola smiled you could see twelve teeth in her upper jaw. Me, eight.

I flipped the sun visor down and flashed a smile at the mirror. Still eight. I had my father's small mouth. I flipped the visor up. I couldn't bear another look.

Van gunned the engine.

'Watch out,' he said with a grin. 'The horses in this thing'll give you whiplash.'

We zoomed away from my apartment building.

'I've got the next Brando on my books. You should see this kid.'

'Do I know him?'

'Nah, no one does. I found him at some improv night before I left TI. Jake didn't want him. The kid made me see the light. I got him the lead in the new *Agent Orange* franchise. Chase Cardoso. He's gonna blow up.' He kept talking as we drove too fast down Sunset. The car took curves like a dream.

I didn't much feel like talking, but didn't want to seem sullen.

'Your car is so much fun,' I said, figuring I could interrupt his flow of speech with a car compliment anytime. What had we talked about when he was manning my ex-agent's desk? I couldn't recall. But talking with him had felt good, like anything was possible for him, and so, by extension, for me.

He gave me another blinding smile and looked me in the eye. 'I'm glad you reached out. There was this girl auditioning for a part. Totally wrong for it. They wanted a Louise Brooks type. I don't even know why they brought this one in. But something about her made me think: Echo. I should look that girl up. And there you were in my inbox.' He took his eyes off the road and pointed to his third eye and then to mine. 'What's new?'

His intense, expectant stare. It asked to be impressed.

I had to turn away and squeeze my eyes shut to keep them from spilling: *My father died this summer. He took one wrong step and was gone. Maybe the grip on his sneakers had been worn smooth, or he glanced up from the rocks as he climbed over the sea cave to watch a pelican dive.* Everything inside me, ocean. I inhaled with both my nose and mouth, greedy for air, feeling my lungs expand. My body was mostly water, but only mostly, still.

'I've been modelling,' I said, knowing the way he'd hear it – as far away from standing naked in an art centre for sixty bucks a session as I wished to be. The leather on his dash felt impossibly durable.

He looked me up and down. 'I knew old Jake should have pushed you for more than crack whores and dead girls.'

Silence.

'You know what I mean,' he chuckled.

'Totally.'

'Or…' He took his hands off the steering wheel to make air quotes and the car drifted into the left lane.

I froze.

'The fugly friend. Remember that one?' I didn't like that we were laughing. He was supposed to want to send me out for comedy, for horror, anything. Van put his hands back on the wheel. When he straightened the car out, he oversteered. It wasn't his fault, it was this model.

'I bet you're getting booked for pin-up-type jobs now, huh?'

'Something like that,' I said.

At the next intersection we idled at a red light, and heat built up inside the car. The smell of oiled leather made me feel sick. When the light changed, the car beside us beat us across the large, empty intersection. The road was clear and Van sped up to fifty, giving me a knowing smile. When he slowed to turn a corner, the engine's gruff rumble gave way to percussive pops. I've always loved the sound of an air-cooled flat six.

My dad would tell me that, back in the day, there was nothing else like the 930 Turbo, and the 911 was only ever a tribute to that supercar. *The 911's still as hot as Madonna*, I remember him saying, *but unlike Madonna, it's not the only turbocharged thing on the road anymore.* I felt protective of my pop idol when he talked about her like that, as though what she was doing was for him and not for me. Protective and jealous, and with jealousy came shame, the sense that something was out of place. Was what we wanted from her the same? But Madonna did not need my protection. She was a woman in control, generous with her body, the spectacle of it, the idea of it in dialogue with other bodies, mine. I imagined she didn't think about sex in terms of men or women, but grace, strength, and beauty. I wanted to be part of this. I don't think this is what my father wanted. His desire was clear and common. Mine had a syntax I had yet to discover. And I had to look carefully to see it.

What Dad meant when he talked about those cars was that he wasn't into faddish consumption. He had his Karmann Ghia, and those were wheels you held on to. You don't trade in your first love just because there's a newer model. The three of us took his car up to Monterey. Not every year, but often, me in the back, knees to chin. How hot it could be, even at the coast. My dad always booked the same hotel because my mother never got over how it was owned by her favourite girlhood actor, a cowboy who made her believe that the Wild West in her German books about the Apache warrior Winnetou was at least as real as Neverland. She was so happy on the porch of the ranch house, watching sheep roam the hillside, being somewhere she recognized. June was when he took vacation. June was now gone.

Van squeezed the steering wheel with his right hand, then his left. His gaze wandered up my legs, over a silk slip dress I bought at a consignment store. A timeless wardrobe staple I could hardly afford even then, when I was living off savings from a commercial for a cellular carrier and spent a good part of that year covered in blood or submerged in water in low-budget direct-to-video movies from a production company most famous for always turning a profit. I'd bought the dress because I knew it would serve me well.

'Yup,' he said, running his teeth over his lower lip. 'Too bad Martini already has Lola LaForce.'

He winked. I relaxed. He could see what I was good for.

On a dimly lit street off Sunset we pulled up to a valet stand outside a shoebox building with no windows.

The restaurant was lit like a moonless night. Dark walls and moleskin chairs, electric candles, crocodile tabletops. I ran my thumb along the groove of a scale, waiting as the waiter pulled out my chair. Black napkins, cutlery gleaming.

A man in a suit stepped into a mist of light and said, 'Mr. Waldron, always a pleasure.' A firm handshake. 'Miss,' he nodded at me and smiled so kindly I wished he would feed me under the table.

A waiter filled our champagne flutes.

Soon the small plates started coming: one bite each. 'I took the liberty of ordering,' Van said, and we began eating in silence. I ate slowly, as if the food consumed me. I waited for him to notice. The way I held my fork and knife, not the American way, not the European way, but a hybrid of my parents'. My dad's grip all fist, no matter how he arranged his fingers, my mother surgical. It was never appropriate to ask why my way of eating fascinated the men who took me out on dates, and they never offered an explanation, but their attention made me aware of my power. So I perfected it.

I held my fork in my right hand to cut and to eat. I pushed small bites onto the back of the tines, a lick, a taste of everything. He watched me guide the fork to my mouth. Charred squid, a smear of red pepper salsa, crisp honey-cured bacon. As soon as it was in my mouth, I looked at him. I waited.

'I love watching you eat,' he said.

I smiled as if I had no idea what he was talking about. This was essential: to deny knowledge of my powers. Only then would he feel that finding me was an achievement.

'You're not allergic to anything, are you?' he asked.

'No, no. It's all wonderful.' I said. Scallops kind of grossed me out. Something about the texture. But my father loved them. He would eat them in one bite, wanting all the flavors at once, and chewing slowly. I swirled the fatty creature in the foam and put it in that small mouth.

Van refilled my glass as I chewed.

We were each given a plate of Tournedos Rossini. I hadn't eaten beef since the last time a man took me to dinner.

'Did you know the Savoy created this dish for Rossini himself?' I asked.

'Don't know him.'

'The composer. *Barber of Seville*?'

'I stay at Claridge's when I'm in London.'

'But you know Rossini. Remember the singing frog: *Figaro qua, Figaro la, Figaro su...*'

Van smiled. 'You're a funny girl.'

'It's a funny song.'

I cut into the medallion and the pink juice mingled with the sauce, the glistening crouton, the musky black truffle. I was hungry and considered eating the foie gras, but I pushed it to the side of my plate instead.

He said, 'Yeah, you probably shouldn't eat that now you've got that model body.'

I pinched my thigh under the table. Had grief made me thin? I could never get a read on my body.

'I'm still an actress,' I said.

He waved his hand. 'Right, right. But be careful with what you put away. You've never had a weight problem, but you're not getting any younger. What are you, twenty-four?'

I remembered the age I gave Jake. 'Twenty-two.'

'You watch out for twenty-seven… Girls in this town.' He gestured around his hips. He told me about the agency he had started, the advances he'd been rejecting. He initiated a game of Fuck Marry Kill, which we'd played before, and I stared at my steak. My juicy steak. I wanted to eat it all, but I was afraid he'd think I didn't care about my figure, those three make-or-break pounds, and I wanted him to know that I did care and I had what it took to get on his books, even if this was turning out to be some sort of date. The medallion was about as wide as a tennis ball. I was as hungry as when we arrived. I rolled the wine around the glass.

'Nice legs,' I said, trying to figure out what was the least amount I could eat to show him that I appreciated the food and cared about my figure, and also feel full. He took this as a cue to order a second bottle. I was already tipsy. If I was feeling tipsy, I was probably drunker than I thought I was. I didn't want to be drunk with him. I decided to eat half of the medallion.

When I finished, I put my cutlery down, metal to porcelain, soundless. Pointing the blade of the knife at my dinner companion, always hoping my dinner companion would interpret this as a wink, a gesture of intent.

He said, 'I'm glad you reached out. You're a cool girl. Different.'

I smiled as if no one else had ever told me this. I was still trying to figure out how to get the leftover steak home with me. I looked around the restaurant. It was open-plan and although it was dark, I couldn't talk to a waiter without his noticing, or sneak out a doggie bag. What if I called Orly. Orly. The thought of her confused me.

'What's up, babe?'

Suddenly: *babe*.

I shook my head and gave him a sleepy smile. 'Just,' I said, touching my hair and looking at the room. 'This.'

He took my foie gras, shoved it in his mouth and filled my glass. 'So you like it, huh? They used my interiors guy.'

Dessert arrived. He looked especially pleased.

'It's lavender crème brûlée.'

The waiter walked backwards away from the table.

Van cracked the caramelized crust with his spoon, smashing the flowers into the silky custard. I considered picking up my spoon. I didn't.

'Oh no, babe,' Van said. 'Are you sore about what I said? Look, you might not be a leading lady, but you're pretty. You're the kind of pretty that'll stick. Even when you're twenty-seven.'

I stared at him and smiled, not showing my teeth.

'Go on, you can cheat with me. I won't tell. I like a naughty girl.'

He scooped up a heaping mouthful of crème brûlée and reached it over to me.

'Open up.'

His arms were short, and the hand holding the spoon hovered above my glass. Some lavender dropped into my wine. It sank.

I shut my eyes and closed my mouth over the mound of cream. My lipstick left a red smear on the silver.

VAN CAME BACK FROM his kitchen with two frosty glasses filled with viscous liquor. 'Marty' had taught him how to make them, he said, and I acted impressed. He didn't seem to remember I'd been at that party, too. He had told me to make myself at home, and was now repeating that I should make myself at home. I took off my shoes and tucked my feet under me on the sofa, a tufted leather platform next to a picture window, a gas fireplace, and a small stack of unopened LPS. It was a picturesque place to sit, and I sat up straight, not reaching for the glass, but receiving it. As I drank, I noticed an unboxed record player in the corner.

'My guy at Helix sent it over. We can set it up another day. You seem like a vinyl kind of girl.'

He gazed into my eyes.

'Sure,' I said. His face seemed strained, and it made him look old.

'You, you're spectacular, you know that?' he said with a bashful smile. 'You and me. We could really be something.'

I sipped the drink, unsure of what to say. The old hope came creeping, that something would come of our meeting, that maybe him thinking I was spectacular meant everyone else would too. After all, the Seven Sisters only became stars because Orion was pursuing them.

Out the window, the houses and apartment buildings seemed to be propped up on the sloping road, half-hidden by bushy trees, and beyond their crowns, a sea of light.

'It's good, right? As soon as I saw that view, I knew I wasn't walking away.'

'You see what you want and you take it,' I said.

'Always,' he said, and it was meant to be flirtatious, but it annoyed me. If he was so decisive, why did he insist on ambiguity here? Or was I being stupid? Was he revealing himself to me? I tried to tell myself that it didn't matter, because it wasn't about *me*. It was about my career. Or about finding comfort in the familiar, and together we'd enter into oblivion. Hope was a sort of eclipse. And in its shadow, I would feel my way to orgasm.

'And there's a cherry on top. The pilot for *Asphalt Knights* was written here!'

'I loved *Asphalt Knights* as a kid. Every time I turn my headlights on at sunset, I pretend I'm in the title sequence.'

'You and everyone else. That show is iconic,' he said.

The way the ceiling light was hitting him, I could see the gel in his hair was flaking. And he'd had too much sun, which he couldn't pull off the way Krit did. It jarred with the condo and his pressed shirt. His skin made me think he didn't quite know how to take care of himself. My mother used to show me pictures of bronzed women with skin like a dry lake bed and say, *Sunscreen*, as if it were a command. Her chest would always burn when she lay outside. I never burned. Not even with Orly. It hadn't yet occurred to me that the lack in his appearance wasn't a lack at all, but the beginnings of him not having to care anymore because he was a man on the rise.

'When I sell this place, they're going to say, "Van Waldron lived here,"' he said. 'I know it.' And he went on to tell me about his neighbours, how relieved he was that the streets at the foot of the hill were starting to clean up. The undesirable element. Property value. Location.

'Sounds like you invested wisely,' I said.

'I'm doing all right. It's all about the exit plan.'

The ice rattled in the cocktail shaker as he stirred up another round of drinks. I stared at a star. It seemed too bright for this sky, fat and gleaming. I waited for it to move.

He stepped in the way of my view, with a glass in each hand and his penis hovering near my nose. It was sticking out of his fly. As he moved, it bobbed.

'Suck me,' he said.

I'd been here before.

'I want you to taste me,' he said.

Van stepped closer, it jabbed me under my nose.

'Yeah,' he said as if it had been my idea. 'Taste me.'

He lifted up his shirt and showed off his thick torso. Of all that was speeding through me, my mind rested here: his choice to be hairless was regrettable.

I felt cornered, so I opened my mouth and gave it a suck. A reflex parallel to inaction. The thought that follows: it's already done. Pre-cum on my tongue. I salivated to wash my mouth out. He liked that too.

Van looked over his shoulder at his reflection in the window as he unbuttoned his shirt. I pulled my dress over my head. I'd spent the holiday season wrapping lingerie at a boutique on Melrose where I worked in part because of the discount. Male shoppers stared freely at my breasts as we figured out their lovers' sizes. I wouldn't let them leave without a gift receipt. I was wearing a semi-sheer basque with a matching thong. He buried his face in my cleavage.

I took it as a good sign that I didn't have to ask him to use a condom. It was out and then it was on. The gesture made me want to believe he was a good person deep down, respectful and conscientious. As affable as the person I'd met manning my ex-agent's desk. Part of the effect of hope's eclipse was a tendency toward kind interpretation, but my insistence on looking for the good in people had never served me well. It meant I would bend myself to fit in with them, without considering how I actually wanted to be. Tonight I needed to be spectacular.

Van started to undo his pants, but I told him to keep them on. He liked my assertiveness. As I manipulated him through the fly and fabric, I could see he liked watching me work within my limitations. 'You like that?' I asked again and again; the words were warming him up, the steady climb. I liked watching him cede control and then his will was mine. I pushed my thong to the side. I engulfed him.

The sofa had been cleared of its pillows by the time we were done. Our sweat had begun to irritate his newly waxed skin. His fingers danced on my hips as he whispered *baby baby baby*. I tickled him with my long hair. Careful to hold the condom at its base, I dismounted. He gasped and laughed. I liked him like this. Maybe we *could* be something, I thought. I could be a vinyl kind of girl. Funny, cool, different. Spectacular. His. I could start fresh. I'd work my bra size into the conversation so he wouldn't have any trouble buying me lingerie. I was forever wishing that what I'd lost would come find me. He could be my daddy.

Watery blood had pooled in the folds of the condom. I couldn't remember my last period or having bought tampons in the weeks, months I'd been alone with my mother in my parents' house. How long had it been? I thought what I always thought even though I was careful with protection: another bullet dodged. He reached out to help with the condom.

'Careful,' I said.

He sat up and his latex-wrapped penis flopped on his pale trousers.

'Fuck,' he said, rubbing at the spot. 'Fuck!'

'Hey, Van, hey,' I said. 'I can get that out for you. Easy.' My mother had made me watch when she trained Blanca, so I knew how to get anything clean.

'Oh, you can? How about not putting your shit on my new pants in the first place.'

He didn't push me off him exactly, but when he stood up my shin knocked the heavy coffee table. He didn't care.

'Fuckin'…'

We looked each other in the eye. We both knew that whatever he said next, he wouldn't be able to take back. I'm not sure he minded the blood so much as the stain. No one likes having their new things ruined. I felt ashamed and angry that I felt ashamed because the body will do what it does. But I suppose this evening had never been about our bodies.

He turned and stormed up the stairs to the mezzanine where I could see his bed through the railing. A door slammed. The shower started running. I couldn't find another bathroom. In the kitchen, I cleaned myself up with a wet paper towel and threw it away in the trash can under the sink. I tore off another couple of sheets, folded one and stuffed it between my legs. The other, I wanted to put in my clutch just in case, but I couldn't get a handle on the clasp. It fell from my shaking hands, and the crash of hard resin and its clatter against the tiles made me feel jagged. I didn't want to wait around for him to call me a cab. It was wishful thinking that he would.

I COULDN'T GET CELL reception outside of Van's house, so I started making my way to the main road. Waving searchlights from the boulevard lit up the clouds. My feet on solid ground.

The hilly neighbourhood looked so much like home – no sidewalks or streetlights, insulated by wealth. Cypress trees. Shrubs. Cracked streets. Old villas with red-tiled roofs. Ornate garage doors. Rusted pick-up overhung with angel's trumpets. And that was it. I was in a cul-de-sac. I turned around and tried another street.

A flight of stairs ran between the houses, and I thought it might be a shortcut. At the landing, there was a white gate. Beyond the gate, a slope. At its foot, headlights glided around the bend. The gate was locked. Impossible to squeeze through or jump. And then I felt foolish for wanting to. It was pitch-dark down there. Dark and silent. I remembered every dead woman I had ever seen on film. Every horror story. I tried to remember the name of the girl who was taken into police custody up in Topanga and released at night without a ride home. She disappeared. Lost in the canyons. A year went by, she was assumed dead, but her father went on the news and pleaded with us to remember her name, to remind us that she was a person, not a story, and she was still missing. I took off my shoes, as if a soundless footfall would protect me. Sprinted up the stairs. Jogged along another road, hoping it would get me off this hill, but it was a dead end, too.

I was sweating, which made the cool night too cold. I should have taken a jacket. My dad always told me to take a jacket when I leave the house and to always have a decent pair of shoes at hand. What if your car breaks down? What if you lose your keys?

Of all the things he saw coming, I'm sure he never imagined his daughter like this. I remember him warning me about the 'reach-around.' He set the scene: I'd be on a movie date and the guy would put his arm around my shoulder, hand dangling near my chest. Once we'd settled in, he'd try to cop a feel. No man ever put his arm around me in the movie theatre, but every woman I know has had a penis sprung on her. Was it that my dad came of age in a different time, or did he want to keep the world from me in hopes I'd never find out what he knew? Did he hope – I remembered the dates Ana's parents had started setting up for her as soon as she turned sixteen – I would be quick to find a pure and lasting love, and I'd slide from his care into the care of another, without ever having to encounter these wilds?

I took the next left. The street widened as it wound downhill. The villas gave way to apartment complexes with For Rent signs stuck in patches of thirsty lawn. Soon I saw the main road, but my good feeling was long gone. I hadn't planned on walking tonight or being outside. I wasn't dressed for it. With each step, the edge of the paper towel dug into me. I kept reaching under my dress to make sure it wasn't slipping. A pert buzz from my phone. If it was Van, I didn't want to know.

Behind me, a pair of headlights flashed. I looked back and saw a car making its way toward me. I walked faster toward the main road, where there were lights and people. I tried to ignore it. I tried to stop my thoughts. The what if, what if. A burst of blue light. I stopped. The car pulled up beside me. The driver's window was rolled down.

'I'm sorry, officer,' I said. 'I didn't know… I mean, is something the matter?'

The officer asked for ID. After studying my driver's licence, he said my name and the name of the city out loud. I was still registered at my parent's address. He repeated my last name: Logan.

'As in Jack Logan?'

'Yes, officer.'

'You're the daughter?'

'I'm the daughter,' I said.

'I got a cousin on the Reserve Dive Team.' He sounded apologetic. Rattled, even. I'd only ever known cops to be weary and bored, immovable in their decision to issue me a speeding ticket.

'They did everything in their power – ' he said.

I cut him off, and as soon as I did I realized I probably shouldn't have, but I didn't want his condolences. I said, 'You're all so brave. Thank you,' even though I wasn't grateful. I was disappointed. Angry. I counted four divers that day. I watched them scour the bay. They were in the kelp beds and then by the rocks. After a while all they seemed to be doing was swimming in formation.

In the back of the cop car, I thought I'd lost something. I did my usual check and slid my fingers around the pockets, the lining of my clutch. Cell phone and keys, my ID. Crumpled kitchen towel. I smoothed it out. Nothing. No cash. I felt around the bag again and again. No card. I kept smoothing out the towel, as if the act of smoothing could cause money to emerge, like the live butterfly I'd once seen a magician pull from a drawing he'd made on his skin. But there was nothing. No money at all.

'You all right back there, dear?'

Dear. Even spoken kindly, it carried with it my father's bite. I didn't want to be anywhere near him.

'I'm looking for my lip gloss,' I said.

He chuckled. 'You don't need that gunk, you know.'

'OK,' I said.

He dropped me off near the metro next to the mall on the Walk of Fame. Taxis rolled by.

'You sure I can't drive you home?'

'Yes.'

He nodded at me in the rear-view mirror. I reached for the door handle, but he turned around in his seat so he could look at me. I thought of his lower back, his discs degenerating with each twist, just like my father's.

'If my little girl lost her pops… I think about it all the time.' His eyes were pleading, but I didn't have an answer for him. 'They know what to do if there's a body.'

'If there's a body,' I said.

The silence between us. The ocean a grave. Everything an ocean. No body to bury, his body in the waves.

AS THE COP DROVE OFF, bros on the sidewalk shouted at me and thought they were being cute. A homeless man asked for the time, and when I told him I didn't have a watch, he asked again and again until I told him it was midnight in hopes he'd calm down. He pointed and backed away, shouting that I was a witch. No one seemed to notice.

I considered going to the hotel bar across the street. A tabloid journalist used to take me there when he was tracking a pop star in the middle of a very public nervous breakdown. He said showing up with a girl like me made it easier for him to get into places like these. He bought the drinks and introduced me to people he thought were good to know. Like the bartender, Marty, who Van also knew.

Marty liked trying out his concoctions on us. His homemade bitters and syrups, drinks with balloons that released a citrus essence when you popped them over your martini. *Finally, a girl who can hang*, he'd said about me after hours one night. Marty started inviting me to things. I watched him run through women like I ran through stockings. It was fun until the day he asked me if we were going to 'do this already.' When I tried to remember the look on his face, all I could see was Dr. Moradi. Something sharp entered my heart. I waited until it dulled.

Instead, I went into the mall, a three-storey outdoor shopping complex built to look like the largest, most expensive film set in early Hollywood history. Bright, busy, and clean. I couldn't stand the place, all dressed up to make you feel like you were in the Hollywood of dreams. I didn't like the lie. I found a bench and sat down. Beneath reliefs of the Assyrian gods of water and light, cameras flashed as people took pictures of themselves with the

Hollywood sign in the background. The mall's viewing decks spanned a replica of the Babylon Gate, a door that leads to wonder.

Two women stumbled out of the nearby elevators, leaning their weight on two broad-shouldered men. One of the women, her skin and hair and lips glistening, made the group stop in front of me. Her belly pouted in her dress.

'Don't cry,' she slurred. 'Men are buses. Right? There's always lots of fish.' She squeezed the arm of the man she was holding. Military muscle. The other couple was making out. The man was playing grab-ass with her. Maybe that's what my dad had meant. 'You're so pretty!' she said. She was nodding her head while asking the man: 'She's pretty, right?' And then she tugged on the other man's T-shirt. 'Jeff, Jeff.' He ignored her. 'Cyn, Cynthia. Cyn, tell her she's pretty. Isn't she sooo pretty?'

Cyn stopped her kissing and dropped her head back without really looking at me. 'You're soo pretty,' she said as Jeff fixed his mouth to her neck. 'You could have, like, *any* guy you want.'

Cyn worked hard to make that sentence sound sincere, like believing it was a matter of my salvation. Mine and hers. She wasn't wrong. You could have anyone, as long you didn't care how you were wanted. That sharpness again. How different it all could have been.

The women looked at each other, and chimed, 'But not ours!'

There was a buzzing in my clutch. It took me a second to realize what it was.

I laughed along with them just to make them go away. Their men stood there smirking, indulgent. They wrapped their big arms around the girls, swayed down the steps, and disappeared down the sidewalk. Pedestrians flowed around street performers and party-goers posing by the names of their favourite stars spelled out on the sidewalk.

At the foot of the stairs, a neon-haired kid with a reedy voice was singing while a man who looked like he spent his days at Muscle Beach listened intently, hands clasped behind his back, leaning in too close. Naked but for a speedo, a fanny pack, and a pair of hiking boots. The musician held his guitar like a shield. Was my musician alone in that big house, or was he telling another girl about his big plans? I thought about the drive to and from his house, which I'd never do again, and how I should always have my own transportation.

The text messages said: 'What happened?', 'u ok?', and then 'hey.' I deleted them. I scrolled through my phone. I couldn't call any of these people. All these names, none of them friends, really. Not Marty, not Van. Maybe Krit, but I didn't have his number. All the energy I'd expended. I scrolled and scrolled. I kept coming back to Orly's number. Orly, who'd probably never get herself into a situation like this. She'd have put Van in his place and made him pay for her taxi. And if she needed help, she'd ask for it.

On the ground was a concrete trail meant to look like a red carpet leading to that gate of wonder. Inlaid in the trail were testimonies to success by anonymous somebodies and nobodies in the film industry. Key grips and directors. Screenwriters and property masters. A composer's said he had been teaching at UCLA when a producer called, looking for a student to score a sci-fi movie. 'I'll send my best student,' he said, but he sent himself instead. I accepted the blame the story placed on me for standing still.

I looked to the gods on the gate for strength. Their blessing was in everything around me: the terrazzo and brass stars, the crowds, the letters on the hill. And so I did it. I dialled Orly's number.

WHO DID I IMAGINE Orly to be? I knew so little about her, her everyday, what I may or may not be interrupting by calling her late at night. What I did know was how she made me feel. Welcome, all of me. It was a bullet of a thought. Once it entered me, my flesh was changed. Maybe I could ask for what I wanted and not be denied. Maybe to feel the way I felt with her was worth the risk that it might one day end. I had learned to move through life in spite of what hurt, favouring my left side to my right, never bending from the waist. I knew how to find pleasure this way, and I had been happy enough taking the pleasures I could find.

I think sometimes of Casanova, who wondered for whom pleasure was greater: woman or man? Nature can never be unjust, the famous lover writes, so for the pains of pregnancy and the dangers of childbirth, Nature must have compensated women somehow. And so, he suggests, it made her experience of pleasure so great it outweighed the pain. Did my pleasures outweigh the pain? Or were they like plaster, creating an attractive shell? Or had I learned to yield to pain until it could be understood as pleasure? Because I could endure, the absence of pain or discomfort was not a prerequisite for my enjoyment. In his pursuit of pain, was a masochistic man seeking an intensity of pleasure only women can know? If he had the choice, would he, like Casanova, prefer to not be born a woman, for though women's pleasure may be greater, he believed that men have pleasures women cannot enjoy? I don't know. It's suspect to carve up the world along lines of anatomical difference. As if the stories science tells about our bodies aren't subject to change. Casanova was wrong in this respect: nature is neither just nor unjust. She is blunt and indifferent, but she will carry us through if we let her, she will carry as much as she can hold, even in the harshest climates. How fertile amaranth are, able to grow taller than the tallest of men, but in drought this unfading flower can only muster a few inches of height. It was hard to imagine, for grief is a desert island on which it's impossible to take a long view. Perhaps the pleasures only men can enjoy are to do with power, but even that power does not serve men well. My father was always strong. He expected himself to be and so did my mother. Capable. Able to handle what came his way, doing everything he could to shield us from incoming storms. His method was financial security and a house in a good neighbourhood with good schools. My mother resented it when he didn't perform, grew angry when he wavered. Down the cliffs, he showed me a different side, a vision of a life that could be – simpler, closer to the heart. But his vision never came home with us. It was as though he was only able to trespass on joy. And this was how he found his release.

A SEMIANNUAL PLAY PARTY hosted in a dominatrix's warehouse near the airport soon after Piggy moved in with Orly. An intimate gathering of clients and friends new and old. Piggy had been saving up for six months to be able to spend time there and have a session.

Last time, Mistress Victoria had worked on him on her own. She said her arm had gotten tired and suggested that not one, but two women should work on him with two floggers at the same time. This arrangement might deliver the intensity of sensation he had called out for. Laughing, she said she needed to save some energy for her other clients at the party. 'I've never seen a man your size take so much,' she'd added, and it made him feel proud. When Mistress Victoria and Lady Sabina were done, he fell into a sort of trance there in her lap, his head in Victoria's hands as she stroked him over the ears, humming, and when he put his button-down shirt back on, his pants over his leather thong, belt, socks, and lace-up shoes, he sat at the bar for an hour, his body a sound-proof shell, nursing a tumbler of Scotch, and then he got in his car and drove home to Orly. Her very presence was a mercy. It meant everything to him that she was there.

After a session as intense as this had been, he needed time before he reentered the world, and he felt too fragile to meet up with his friends at the all-night diner after the party was done. He loved the community he had finally found, but he was still a loner. It took him time to process what came up when he entered a submissive state beyond his threshold for pain. He thought of it as free-falling inside himself. It left him feeling vulnerable, like looking into the mirror on LSD had – an encounter from which no part of him could hide.

Piggy sat between Orly's knees in the morning, after he'd taken a bath. Bath and Bach, his post-session ritual. The music was still playing. Orly was using his special salve, made from a base of arnica. He kept it for himself, but he'd blend her a batch when she asked. She kept one hand resting on his forehead, her pinky stroking him at his hairline, which had receded somewhat since they'd first met. Orly knew he was tender, that this grip made him hold still. Orly dipped a finger in the pot and smeared the cool cream along each abrasion. There was no rush. It was as much about care as it was about touch. He kept his eyes closed, mind full of music, the sound of her fingers on his skin, the pressure of her knees. The two of them together, breathing out and in. In these moments, he felt whole and calm.

When Orly was done, they sat together for a while, by the open window, the breeze blowing in a direction that brought the sound of the ocean inside. She asked him to face her. He kneeled, but she asked him to sit. She wanted them to be eye to eye.

'I met someone,' she said.

And he knew she meant the neighbour girl. Orly was on the sofa where the girl had slept. Strange to see the girl inside, in his home. He'd waved at her every day and the gesture had seemed to frighten her. He'd taken it as a good sign. Orly had chosen a location where people weren't interested in being neighbours. But then she'd appeared on Orly's sofa, and he'd rushed out of the house on his way to work, not wanting to wake her.

'We didn't talk about this,' Orly continued. 'What would happen if we brought people over who we didn't already know. I told her what I do, but I left you out of it.'

'Thank you.'

'Of course.'

Piggy thought about his separate lives. His office jobs, his service to Orly. The distance he enforced between himself and his work colleagues, never letting them get too close unless he trusted them to be in his inner circle. He had enough friends now who shared his interests. He was too old to watch his mouth during his leisure time. When he felt social, he wanted to be able to make jokes at his own expense and trade tales of mishaps on the road to getting here in the same breath as he explained the perfect blend for burger meat at a barbecue. He had spent too long holding back and keeping things down.

'You must really like her.'

'More than I think I was prepared to.' Orly paused. 'She's going through a lot.'

Something dropped inside him, and the words came out harsher than he expected: 'Not another project.'

Orly looked hurt. 'This isn't like Kashmira. I took her on because she said she wanted to learn from me. Echo, she interests me. I wonder what she'll be like if we play.' She squeezed her eyes shut and smiled.

He didn't want to encourage her fantasy about this new girl. When she dreamed, it was potent, easy to get swept away. Part of her genius, he thought, was her imagination, but when she fantasized, she also lost her connection to the world around. He wanted her to stay with him in this conversation. He thought about Kashmira, who had been her assistant a few years before. Initially sweet, and eager. But when Orly let her get more and more involved, taking over the sessions Orly was supposed to do with him, he felt left behind. And then it became clear that Kashmira only thought about the money: she had seen what Orly had and wanted it for herself. She didn't care about the work, the connection. She began poaching Orly's clients, using Orly's name as a reference, without her blessing. And one day there was no

Kashmira anymore. Orly had asked him not to stay in touch with her at least for a while, as a courtesy. Thinking about the possibility of another girl spending time with Orly in the house – another project girl – it occurred to him that his hurt about Kashmira was really about something else. He said, 'You're supposed to protect me.'

He liked the way Orly listened. Taking in his every word.

'You're right,' she said. 'I promise I won't be careless.'

THE SECOND TUESDAY of the month. Piggy's regular day of service. His day of days. A day around which all else revolved.

In the morning, he fixed her coffee and brought it to her in bed. Orly assessed his work and then dismissed him. She brushed her teeth and put on a kimono a client had bought her when she was working from Japan, and met Piggy in the living room. There he was waiting with the locked box in which his rope was kept. His rope, a rope he cared for, a rope for him to keep clean and in good shape. She'd chosen it for him. Superman red. She'd said: *Star Sapphire seized control of Superman by hanging her gem around his neck. I'm going to make you a harness. When you wear it, your will is mine.* She draped the rope around his neck and tied the first knot at his sternum.

To mark the start of the session today, Orly would ask him to kneel. Knees spread, naked but for his leather thong, back of his hands resting on his knees, palms up, ready to receive, eyes down. After years of service, he had learned to be comfortable in his body. Undressed, it no longer made him feel ashamed in front of Orly. She spoke the words she used to call him into service, he responded with his words of devotion and submission, and then she took out his rope. Silken and red. She draped the rope around his neck and tied the first knot at his sternum. Then she fashioned a harness of knots criss-crossing his chest and running between his legs, exerting pressure on his balls as he went about his day. With a loose collared shirt, you almost couldn't see it, and it was one such shirt he wore when he ran her errands, starting at the dry cleaner's and ending at the grocery store so the perishables wouldn't spend too long in the car.

On this occasion, she'd asked for something more. Her last client was to leave at eleven p.m., and she wanted Piggy to clean up after him. Normally she kept her clients out of each other's sight, keeping a separate intimacy for each. He knew he was lucky that she had a found a role for him to play in her fantasies, that of her loyal houseboy.

Eleven fifteen, he walked through the door to her playroom. They were alone, so he wore only the harness and his thong. With her, he didn't hate the way his muscles seemed to be lifting from the bone; dips of flesh and papery skin somehow meant nothing with her. He was perfect as Piggy. And she was sublime to him. They'd known each other since she was starting out – perhaps time and proximity were making way for romantic love. He knew it was not part of their agreement, but he'd never stopped hoping.

He stepped on something sharp and hard. Piggy jumped, squealed, and grabbed his bare foot to see what manner of thing it was. Clothespins. Some in piles, others scattered. When he looked up from the floor, he saw her. She had chosen to spend the last part of her day with him. He did not hide his elation, and he thought he saw her smile.

'There are one hundred clothespins,' Orly said. 'Put them in the bucket and clean them. We'll begin there.' A blue plastic bucket, the kind children take to the beach, was in the middle of the room.

From her chair, Orly watched him crawl across the floor on hands and knees, searching under the toy chest and the rest of the furniture, aware of each hair on his body, the way his muscles moved, how little of his skin was covered. He hoped it pleased her to see his body, to see him on hands and knees. It must have. There were other places to sit in view of him, but she had chosen the throne – a high-backed leather and oak chair he'd found at a flea market the week after she'd asked what he thought about being her renter. The rent would be cheap in exchange for help around the house, help that was separate from the hours he spent in her service, this she'd made clear. He sent her a picture of the chair along with his yes. It pleased her and her pleasure was his joy.

And tonight he knew it would be easy to displease her. In the dim, warm light, he saw her hands squeezing the armrest, squeezing, releasing. A sign of impatience and fatigue. He knew she'd had a long day, and yet she was here. It made him feel wanted and special, worthy of the attention of a woman like her. A woman with such beautiful hands, slender and strong, the elegant taper of her fingers. He longed to be asked to kiss each and every one. But without her invitation, there would be no kissing, and so he turned his desire to the clothespins. Doing exactly as she asked. No mistakes. Perfect. Like the work he'd done as part of their renter's agreement.

Orly hadn't wanted to invite any clients in before her sanctuary was complete, and they'd come to a standstill over the cage she wanted to hang in the corner. The ceiling was too weak for suspension points, but he'd found an alternative: building a custom wooden frame, tall and wide enough for most purposes. Solid handiwork. She'd said so. He'd had help, but sometimes help was what was needed to deliver the desired result. It was one of the things he liked about this world: skill sharing. Carpentry, nursing, first aid, the art of Florentine cross-flogging: the community was stronger when this information was shared. And yes, when Orly wanted to be able to suspend people from the ceiling, he called the handiest guy he knew, a general contractor who was also in the scene.

Orly had been so impressed with his work that she'd given him an extra special treat.

Taking her time.

Binding his balls with a cotton lace.

Nice and tight.

Swell and pool.

Dark and hard.

Thrum of pain, twitch.

The ping-pong paddle.

That's what you get for being a good boy.

When the clothespins had been left to dry, he cleaned the bondage table with soap and hot water, finishing with hospital-grade wet-wipes. As he sterilized the surfaces, he couldn't stop himself from thinking it.

How nice this was.

Just the two of them.

In the half-year leading up to this move, when she was busy building her business, and on the road for work, Orly would attend to him over the phone. Trading his services for her time was the only way he could afford it. He knew he wasn't like other clients who had money to burn, offering lavish gifts and cash in tribute. He'd always had to scrimp and scrounge to see her, and after the financial crisis, even those dollars dried up. She had offered him this arrangement, and he felt flattered by her trust. He tried not to be picky about how she handled the exchange. How many days of service had he passed all alone, his only reward a text message, voicemail or a handwritten note thanking him for his work, criticizing it and issuing instructions for punishments he had to carry out on his own? Orly's refusal to be available to him when he craved her the most had felt like part of the tease. Reminding him that he *was* just her plaything. Denial kept him attentive, devoted, and engaged. Sometimes he simply missed her.

As the months wore on, he began to worry that Orly would never have time for him in-person again. He respected the work she put into developing her mail-order business, premium video content, taking care of emails, admin, and herself. He tried not to be greedy, allowed his needs to be subsumed by hers. All he wanted was for her to thrive. Why else would he dedicate so much of his time to her? But he wanted Orly in the flesh, too. She was the keeper of his greatest pleasures. He was devoted to Her.

His goddess.

His queen.

She who is to be admired but not touched.

Sensed but not felt.

His lust could be invoked but not unleashed without her permission. He couldn't always keep it in, and sometimes he'd wake to find his sheets wet. He'd text her an update. Once she'd instructed him to lick it up because everyone knows 'all good piggies are clean.'

He thought of that text often.

The sweet indignity.

No one understood him like she did.

If she wasn't there to watch him come – and when she watched, she watched with glee, peppering the moment with insults, sometimes ruining it all together, cutting his orgasm short, *oh* – he'd write an email from his special account detailing the texture and taste of his cum, what he'd been thinking and feeling, what had pushed him over the edge.

A roll of toilet paper landed at his feet.

He stopped cleaning.

'What happened here?'

He watched her watching him as he picked up the roll from the ground. Holding it close. Squeezing it. A powdery scent.

Scented.

Orly hated scented toilet paper.

'My pussy already smells like peach,' she'd said the last time this happened.

His hands sweated into the soft roll. In the aisle at the grocery store. A child screaming on the floor, a helpless raging thing. He'd grabbed the first paper he had found. Stupid. Stupid. Stupid mistake. He trembled as he told her.

'Come over here,' she said. Kind, but firm.

OK. Better.

She was in the bathroom.

He came.

Head down.

She was sitting on the edge of the tub.

'Sweet Piggy…'

He perked up. She called him by their name.

'Be more careful next time. You know I can't stand sloppy mistakes.'

He nodded.

'You're safe here. Do you understand?'

He didn't respond. It seemed too much right now, to feel like this, to be like this with her, welcome and heard. If he moved, if he opened his mouth, he was afraid something would change.

'Say it.'

He did as he was told: 'I understand.'

She thanked him. He had done well tonight. Gone above and beyond. Her smile was warm; she seemed to relax. He blushed.

She took off her shoe, her foot red where the straps had been tight, pushing him away, her foot on his chest.

Allowing him to touch.

Fingers between her toes, chipped red polish. Rolling her ankle in circles. Should he, could he ask to kiss the tips of her fingers and her toes?

'I don't know what I'd do without you.'

Sitting so his face could be closer to it.

Her hum of approval.

His kneading, her pleasure.

Him and her, like it had been at the start.

When she was a novice and he was her only toy or test dummy.

Her cell phone rang.

She gave him a conspiratorial smile.

When she said 'hello,' the word belonged to their moment.

Her foot in his mouth, toes gripping his bottom row of teeth. She put her finger to her lips. He nodded. He would make no sound. With pleasure, he'd suffer in silence.

'No, I'm not busy,' she said for his benefit, wiggling her toes on his tongue.

The voice on the other end, an insistent staccato buzz.

She turned away from him to listen.

Her toes stopped moving in his mouth. Her foot was heavy. She pulled it out.

'Of course. I'll be right there.'

That sinking feeling.

Could it never be just the two of them?

PIGGY IMAGINED ORLY driving away: along the road that ran parallel with the coast. When he'd first driven down here, when she'd asked if he'd like to see the space she was planning on renting, he thought he was driving into a resort. To be so close to the sea, free of the city's sounds, no crowds. The word 'dignity' had come to mind. Orly was restoring his dignity, he thought. He looked at the clock by his bed and put his book aside. He was in no state to be reading. He smoothed his hand over his robe, lay flat on the bed, and shut his eyes. He wanted to stay with her.

She'd be at the harbour by now, approaching the freeway, then driving past the shipping containers and the refinery, its red lights blinking against the night sky. And on to downtown. He wondered if she had put some music on, if she was thinking of him, the classical station, maybe, or the mix he'd made her. If she was listening to the music, was she looking forward to picking up where they'd left off before the neighbour girl interrupted them with her phone call?

He checked the time. She'd be coming into downtown where the traffic would be clogged, it always was. Maybe she'd anticipate it and take the surface streets. He listed the most likely options, picturing her car moving along, stopping at red lights or catching a good flow. Her car was clean. Spick and span. He'd had it detailed himself. She'd have a chance to enjoy how clean it was, driving on her own, nothing asking for her attention but the road. The leather oiled, the carpets freshly shampooed. The coconut scent she liked. He'd found a good car wash not too far from their house. That morning, after he'd brought her her coffee, he'd watched through the window as the car entered the tunnel to be cleaned. It slid between the spinning brushes, their dull rhythmic thud on its body. He remembered how Mistress Victoria had bound his wrists to the spreader bar, Mistress Victoria and Lady Sabina finding their rhythm, the leather tails spinning in their hands. The wet curtain of fabric strips gliding heavily across the hood of the car had given him the chills. He pictured the car gleaming, his own mistress inside. He checked the time. He guessed she wouldn't park. He guessed she'd pull up to the curb and the neighbour girl would jump in. Orly wouldn't want to hang around, he thought. She'd want to come back to him. She hadn't told him to wait up. But she hadn't told him to go to bed. He checked the time again. She had to be on her way back home.

Sleep came for him. He woke to a low rumble, the car pulling onto the driveway. He checked the time. They must have made a stop along the way. He got out of bed and opened his bedroom door, bleary-eyed but eager to greet her. He heard Orly talking with someone as she entered the house. The neighbour girl. Laughing as they made their way to the stairs. He quietly shut his door. He listened to the women walk down the hall, Orly opening the linen closet to take out a fresh set of towels. The sound of water running, and then nothing at all. He waited.

Then he crawled into bed, hoping sleep would find him again. It did not. So he did what he could to still the large feeling that made your desire seem both within reach and beyond your grasp. There was nothing he could do until morning. And his mornings with Orly had a fixed routine. He saw no reason to hide in his own home.

ORLY BUNDLED ME into her car like precious cargo.

I could, if I dared, choose feeling.
 We hit our speed on the freeway and the light began to stream.
 She ferried me past the bends.
 We rode the tide.
 Her hand on the wheel, her hand on my thigh.
 I could, if I dared, choose feeling.
 A texture inside.
 Filling.

Orly took her hand from my thigh to set the parking brake. Where her hand had been was smoldering. She made a show of unbuckling me, pressing her finger down. I watched her watch the hard edge of the seat belt slide along my neck; it was holding me in place. How thin the skin was there.

'Do you want to come in?' she asked, as if she couldn't have predicted my reply.

Orly's house was silver in the moonshine, its votive glitter on the waves. Light clung to the jasmine and honeysuckle climbing the trellis at the front of her house. The garden respired. The roses were slack with the weight of their curving scent. A breeze rustled the pygmy palms, their heavy swaying fronds. Root and soil, the underside of leaves. Where light will not reach. All is well and all else forgotten. Open your lungs and breathe.

ORLY SAID SHE'D WAIT while I showered.

Only when I was in the bathroom did I realize she'd followed me in.

'Do you mind if I watch?' she asked.

I shook my head but turned to the side, wanting her to see but unsure if she'd like what she saw. I was still dolled-up for someone else. I snuck a glance at her in the mirror. She was leaning against the doorframe. Content.

I discarded the dress.

The undergarments.

The paper towel stiff with blood.

I flung them into the corner by the toilet.

When my shoes were all that was left to remove, she said, 'Let me see.'

I struck a pose. Fists to hips.

'Lovely,' she said. 'Turn around.'

I spun with Orly as my point of focus, and then kicked off my shoes so they landed at her feet. One, two. My dexterous toes.

The full costume on the floor.

In the shower I scrubbed and scrubbed my skin. Scrubbed away the sweat, mine and his, sweat from the seat of the cop car. I scrubbed away everything that had touched me. I rinsed away the musk of bleeding. All that I was shedding. She reached through the curtain and touched my lips. My mouth opened. Water rained in.

When I was done, she wrapped me in a towel. The scratch of terry cloth, softening as it dried my hot skin, slightly sore. She ran the towel up my legs, my torso, cupped my breasts and squeezed. Without meaning to, but meaning it fully, I said, 'Thank you.'

She laughed and squeezed me again. This time I moaned to show her I liked it. To show her how much I wanted her, I did all the things I knew how to do. Moving in ways I knew to be pleasing. Arching my back and pressing my bottom against her. My bare, clean skin against the towel against her body. The cushion of her breasts. When she didn't respond, I noticed my expectation. I was waiting for her cue: indications of pleasure that would let me know how to proceed. When I was done, she would think I was spectacular.

'Stop,' she said.

I froze. Maybe it was still early enough to pretend we'd never seen each other like this. Maybe we could go back to being just neighbours in a community that didn't act like a community unless something was spoiling the view. We'd wave at each other on the street, nothing more. I was hiding myself with my arms.

'This isn't going to work if you're afraid to look at me,' Orly said.

Her eyes were kind.

'I want you,' she said.

'I'm on my period,' I said.

'I don't mind.'

With one finger, she unfastened my towel and let it drop.

My hair was dripping wet. She watched a droplet roll down my torso and then erased its path with her thumb. I sucked it.

She held me close. I stiffened; she held me tighter and murmured, 'Don't move a muscle.'

She let me go.

I breathed in sips until I seemed not to be breathing at all. I stood still. She dragged her thumbnail down my chest, where the drops were falling. Leaving marks. White from the pressure, then red. Lines that faded slowly. She commented on how they shifted and changed. Paying close attention. She studied the effect of her actions, refining them until I was no longer cold. From jaw to shoulder. From collarbone to hip. Dip of the neck to navel. Hip to thigh. She noted every shift in my breath, every hair raised, how and when the goosebumps spread. She dragged her nail across my breasts and my body rolled toward her. There was nothing I could do to stop it.

I tried not to blink.

Her brutal hands. The pain glowing, the heat rising. Trying to keep still. The awareness again of blood rushing, breath quickening. Pulsing, expanding, contracting, wet. Everything she conjured in me, rushing to appear. There was nothing else I could do. I surrendered myself to her.

She brushed her hand across my torso, as if wiping a window clean. The deepest breath, a sigh.

'Show me more,' she said.

The lines she had traced caught fire, and I followed the path of the hottest flame. Raised like a scar. I pressed my finger against it, trying to discern an edge, finding it with my fingernails. I pressed, and with a sensation like stumbling in your sleep, my finger slipped under the skin. There was an opening. I felt queasy, then curious. What would I be without this skin? It didn't matter. I wanted her to have what she was asking for. I wanted more.

Slowly, I pushed my finger further in. Splitting warp and weft, a tear. Offering little resistance. I tore open the seam from elbow to shoulder. Our eyes met, giddy.

She wanted more.

I slipped my arm out of its sleeve. Light flooded the room. Sun on sea, a glister.

'Keep going,' she said.

I pushed my whole hand under the skin of my breasts and peeled my torso clean. It didn't hurt; it was a relief. There was enough room for me. I worked faster and faster, tearing off long, wide strips, tossing them to the floor. The other arm, my legs, face and hair. The spaces between my toes were tricky, as were the backs of my ears, but every inch came off.

I showed myself to her. Sparkling.

But it didn't feel like enough. I wanted to give her more, but no touch no breath no kiss no closeness would be close enough. That insufficient wish: 'I want to be inside you.' I wanted to merge.

I searched my body, my hands playing in the light and waves. Sun on the horizon, stars rising. There was movement inside. A tide. I sunk my hands down into me and raised them up in offering. Drink of me, salt and sweet. Her lips parted in my palms. The way her throat moved. She drank and drank and it wasn't just water she was drinking. She was swallowing my heart.

THE NIGHT SEEMED TO never end. Dressed in dreams, tongues and talk until the sun rose. She held me from behind. We pressed ourselves into each other.

My heart in her chest, beating against my back. Her every breath a vibration. I listened. I felt it racing. Impossible, I thought, that we were sharing space and emotion.

I slept and woke and she was still beside me. The tug of my heart, the thread between us taut and winding. Cocooned in the covers. Was this what it felt like to be safe? I resented the world for its intrusions. I didn't want anything to lay itself over the night. No palm trees or street sounds. No airplanes flying low along the cliffs. No new impressions. I wanted the process of memory-making to stop.

Only her.

Only this.

Only now.

ORLY'S HOUSEMATE WAS ALREADY in the kitchen by the time we got up. He was hand-grinding the coffee when we came in. A carton of eggs and bread were on the counter. Lonnie wasn't quite as old as my dad had been, but the sight of a man with graying hair busy in a kitchen reminded me of the Sundays my dad woke up with a hankering for pancakes and made us tall stacks with a side of fruit and yogurt.

'Hungry?' he asked, and before I could answer, Orly said: 'Don't you have to get to work?' Their eyes locked, and he stepped away from her, wrapped up the bread and put the eggs in the fridge.

'I've got a late shift today,' he replied in a breezy tone that seemed forced. 'Coffee?' he asked.

'Of course,' she said, impatiently.

I didn't know how to read Orly: if she hadn't had enough sleep or if she didn't want Lonnie to fix us breakfast because she didn't want me hanging around. I was about to say goodbye and go home, but then she turned to me and asked: 'How do you take yours?' She sounded formal, and resigned.

Lonnie seemed easily overwhelmed, so I said: 'Black.' Orly pulled out my chair and when I sat, she ran her hand over my hair and I pressed my head into her palm. When she took her hand away, she seemed different, our connection dropped.

Orly took a seat across from me at the small table, which was set for breakfast. The presentation was flawless. The cutlery was parallel and polished. The glaze of the white ceramic plates was uneven and gave the material a sort of glow. As the coffee percolated, Orly's housemate cleared what was not needed from the table. He poured me a cup of coffee, and then began to fix Orly's. The milk, hot from the stove, was poured into a clear tall glass resting on a saucer, about a quarter of an inch. He held the glass low and the coffee pot high and poured, a dark stream. Not a drop was wasted. The milk bubbled and a pale froth formed at the surface. He set the coffee on the table in front of her. She did not drink, nor did she say a word.

'Neat trick,' I said.

'I learned it when I was working at a Mexican restaurant a while back. The owners were from Veracruz.'

I remember the feeling that something didn't fit, a man in my neighbourhood talking about shift work. I wondered what had gone wrong for him, to be so far along in life and still renting, and not even renting but subletting. What good was a man like him, I thought. I was stunned by my harsh assessment. It seemed independent of me. Did I envy him for being at home here? There was more to it. I was looking at Lonnie with my parents' eyes. I remembered Vee, my mother's cat, old and infirm, dragging its body around our backyard. Someone walking along the cliffs didn't have their dog on a leash and it slipped through the fence. I remember the dog, its fervour, its drive. How meek the cat, not vital enough and so it must die. The fur on the lawn. I couldn't run down the stairs and out the door fast enough to stop it.

He kept talking. It put me ill at ease. Orly regarded him coolly, but she didn't interrupt. 'I've had the honour of bringing Orly her coffee every day for almost a decade now. Every morning before nine,' he said.

I resented the tenderness in his voice, and that this was how I was finding out what kind of fixture he was in her life. I wished she would have said something before the three of us met.

'Piggy was my first client,' she said. Her correction would have made me feel better, but I was thrown by the new name.

Orly looked at me and then through me. He never took his eyes off her. She explained: 'Piggy spends some of his time as my houseboy. Bringing me coffee, running my errands. And for now, he's subletting from me.'

Whatever swagger he'd had dissipated when she said 'for now.' I thought about the dog.

Matter of fact and still looking in the distance, she said: 'My coffee's getting cold,' and Piggy leapt into action, fortified by the task.

From one of the wooden drawers, Piggy took a strip of colour swatches in milky coffee colours: cappuccino, latte, mocha. Orly received them and made a show of comparing the numbered colours to the liquid in her cup.

'An improvement,' she said, and set the swatches on the table. He picked them up and put them away.

'I switched to whole milk,' he said. 'It gives a better colour.'

She said: 'Thank you, Piggy.' Then: 'No more today.'

His face fell, and his voice broke when he said: 'Yes, mistress.' He looked like he knew he would be scolded, and I liked that Orly had the decency not to do it in front of me.

Orly took her coffee to the living room and turned on the TV with the news. Clear skies, seventy-five degrees by the beaches. The TV anchors chattered. Meth house raided. Hikers lost in the desert. Amber alert for a nine-year-old boy. A tiger cub smuggled into the state finds a permanent home.

Piggy finished cleaning the kitchen. The milk pan, the coffee machine. As he cleaned, he talked about coffee. How coffee was their first agreement. No matter what, he'd bring her one, even when she was on the road. He'd prepare coffee at home or pick one up to-go and send her a picture. Sometimes he'd leave a voice-mail or send a gift card. How roasts and milk fat percentages impact the colour, how he balances colour with taste. He spoke in clear, fully formed sentences. He seemed practiced in explaining himself. But it didn't feel like a conversation. The answers he gave to my questions were ready-made. He kept glancing at Orly in the living room, distant and removed. I felt an obligation to be polite. It would have been impossible to join her on the sofa and sit with her as though he weren't there. The tension between them made me feel like a child, and I wanted to go home.

MY PARENTS' HOUSE was silent. The windows were open. I watched the ocean heave, all it contained hidden. An ashtray was on the coffee table, but the house didn't smell of cigarettes. I wondered if, in spite of the smoking, my mother was out of her haze. I wished she'd run me a bath again. I smoked some of the pot Orly had given me, and then it didn't hurt so much to look out the window. I thought of Orly on the sofa, I thought of us together. What she did with her clients shouldn't matter to me, she'd made it sound like a clean deal, but Piggy made it messy, like the musician made it messy, and I was left wanting. I checked my phone. No messages. The door to the garage opened.

'Mom?' I called.

It was Blanca. She was carrying in cleaning supplies.

I walked over to her and she hugged me. She squeezed my arms and said: '*Ya come algo.*'

'I eat.'

'Eat more,' she said. 'Where's your phone?'

I patted the back pocket of my jeans.

She shook her head. 'Does it ring?'

I looked away.

'You have people who love you, and when you don't pick up, they worry. I worry, *mijita.*'

She'd always known how to talk to me.

'*Querida,*' she continued. She wouldn't have had to say anything more. I recognized her tone. I knew what was coming. '*Tu mamá no se encuentra bien.*'

The last time my mother was 'not feeling well,' my father wasn't here either. After the unrest that came with statements such as

'This isn't what I signed up for,' and 'Pull yourself together,' he moved out for a trial separation. He was gone for months, a forever amount of time for a child.

One day he'd had enough. I wasn't sure what made Dad hit his limit. I'd heard them scream at each other, seen things break, worse, and that had turned out fine. Within days we'd be back to normal, home-cooked dinners, tennis lessons, and weekend trips where we stopped off to eat pea soup on our way home from touring a castle built by a newspaper man up the coast. But this: this great sadness seeping from my mother – a sadness that made the sky flat and turned the palm trees black – was different. In sickness, in health, in rage, but not in sadness. It was too much for him. That's what he said.

When my dad was loading his suitcase into the car, I took the suitcase I kept packed in case of a fire and sat in the passenger seat of his convertible, refusing to be left behind. Angry, then in tears, then angry again. Maybe this was why he wouldn't let me come with him: I was too much, too. I was still small enough then for him to be able to pick me up and carry me to the living room when his words failed to move me. Blanca arrived the next day with her own bag. She stayed a while, telling me as often as I needed to hear it: 'It doesn't mean he doesn't love you.'

Blanca sat by my bed at night, because I was afraid that if I fell asleep, I would wake up changed, like my mother. Who knew if she'd ever go back to normal. By the time Mom finally started appearing in the hours I was awake too, when she started waking up early enough to take me to school, a lifetime had passed. It was a time I recalled only in fragments, over Blanca's shoulder, my ear pressed to her waist, everything muffled by the rustle of her clothing, her pulse. Her insistence that I eat something. I ate.

My mother wasn't feeling well.

My father was gone.

Blanca had a family of her own.

This is what I knew of love.

My mother wasn't feeling well, and in her barbed way she had asked me to come home. As I knocked on my parents' bedroom door, I thought of Orly's stern silence and how Lonnie had become Piggy, a man in her service. The intimacy in that constant, steady act of bringing Orly coffee every morning, even when she refused to return what looked like love. His actions weren't necessarily a sign of weakness, I thought; perhaps they were a kind of armour.

'I told you: *No hoy,*' I heard my mother say from her bed.

'Mom, it's me.'

Her shutters were closed and the lights were off, but there it was. Salt and sour. I didn't need light to see it: the thickness of her tears. Lips wet, eyes leaking, sniffing the snot back in when she didn't have a tissue. Giving up on having tissues and using whatever was within reach – sleeve, arm, pages of a magazine.

I sat on the edge of the bed and patted the mounds of blankets and pillows, searching for the woman they contained. I found her back, her dainty bones, and felt her body expand and contract. The blankets shifted, and her face appeared. I noticed I was holding my breath, afraid of what would come next: teeth or tenderness. She draped her arm over her eyes as though even the darkness were too bright, and said, 'You're home.'

'Mhm. I got your message.'

'And so you came.' She sounded daft and happy, didactic. 'Sometimes, *schatz*…' From under her arm, she gave me that look of hers, one of deep concern, as though I might already be too far gone, but only maybe. With her wisdom I could be saved.

'You need to be reminded of how to be there for people, don't you?'

When she was down, all she had – and all she ever seemed to want – was me. It was too much to bear. Each word she spoke was a stone in my pocket. Each sentence a step toward the sea. I wanted to let her drown. I wanted to drown. I wanted to show her how to float, if only I knew how. I wanted none of it.

She stroked my arm, as though she felt sorry for me, for my failings. With each second I grew colder, and then she gave my arm her 'that's enough now' pat, as though I had asked for this.

She wasn't oblivious, my mother. No. Maybe she couldn't pinpoint where things were going wrong, but I knew she could feel the distance between us, too wide to see across. She did what she could to close the gap. But I knew better than to trust it to hold.

'Do you remember our trips up the coast? Do you remember what I was like then?' she said, shutting her eyes. She sounded small. I didn't reply. She seemed to fall back asleep, letting out a gentle snore, which roused her. She opened her eyes, shut them. The bottles of pills on her bedside table.

I watched her for a while. Her breathing was light and even, and sometimes she stuttered. When my mother's breathing became heavy, I tiptoed around the room as quietly as I could, picking up glasses that smelled of alcohol, and plates, used tissues, nudging the piles of clothing and file folders strewn across the floor – it looked as though she were in the middle of a project, but it was impossible to imagine her being in the middle of anything but this. I thought about what Orly had said about wanting to help people avoid unnecessary pain, but what happened when the pain became an essential part of you? What did it mean to end it? I was helpless when faced with my mother. I could do nothing about her wounds.

My mother might not have been feeling well, as Blanca had said, but I thought: *This is how it's always been*. When Mom asked if I remembered what she used to be like, this is what I thought of – a dark room, walls with no doors. I didn't know what was worse: that she used to be someone else or that this is what had become of her.

I went upstairs and opened the pantry. Those cluttered shelves. Bags and boxes of crackers and chips made for dip. All bought when Dad was still around, bought for us, so we'd have it around. Jam not yet mouldy. Peanut butter. *Ya come algo.* I mashed a fistful of corn chips between my teeth, comforted by crunch and carbohydrate. The rubber band from around the bag was still intact. I grabbed another fistful. This is how I ate when I was younger. I spit the mush out in the trash. If I was going to eat, I should eat properly. Get a grip. Have a meal. I took a casserole from the freezer. I heated it up. I had it as a late lunch. A reasonable portion doubled. I smoked, I napped, I had more casserole straight from the baking dish and cleaned up after myself. I felt sick.

I went to my room and stayed there, listening to the vacuum cleaner stutter across the floor overhead. I had a new message. Van wanted to talk. His last text read: 'I was trying to impress you. Did I come on too strong?' Bullshit, I thought. I shoved the phone under my pillow.

My phone buzzed and buzzed again. I took it out to turn it off, and saw it wasn't Van pestering, but Orly, checking in.

'That got weird,' she wrote.

'A little.'

'You OK?'

I didn't know what to say. I looked at the screen, my thumbs on the keys. I typed: 'Are all your clients in love with you?' But I didn't press send. I didn't want to ruin it.

Then my phone rang.

'If I was outside,' Orly asked, 'would you come and meet me?'

I DON'T KNOW what possessed me. There were so many places we could have gone. There was the mansion that had been converted into a church, with lush gardens and terraced steps leading down to the sea. You only had to jump one fence and there weren't any security lights. We could have lain on the concrete that once had led to a private pier, now in ruins. We could have lain in the dark under the stars and looked at the 'queen's necklace,' the glittering lights of the beach cities set along the bay. We could have named our own constellations like Dad and I used to do. But no.

Orly was in her car when I came out and asked if I could take her around the scenic route. She gave me the keys.

'There's nothing around here,' I said as we pulled out onto the main road. 'It's pretty and quiet, that's about it.'

'It's how I like it,' she said. 'So do my clients. One of them nicknamed my house "The Resort."'

'That's accurate,' I said. 'But resort life isn't life.'

'One of them told me he feels good coming somewhere nice. It makes him feel like what we do isn't a *dirty* secret.'

The way she looked at me made me laugh.

I decided to ask her: 'Are all your clients in love with you? Or just – ' I hadn't said his name out loud yet ' – Piggy?'

'I'm handling it. He's a romantic, and can get needy. Give him time to adjust.'

'OK.'

'Will you trust me on this?'

I took my eyes off the road to look at her. I would.

We talked as I drove us along the road made bumpy by the constant landslide, up the winding road that led to the top of one of the hills and down again, through canyons thick with eucalyptus trees. The road led past the Moradi house. I couldn't help it. I stopped. Seeing it again, the bitter nostalgia. I unbuckled my seat belt. The pressure of it across my chest and gut was too much. I opened the window a crack and checked the locks. It was a sweet house, ranch-style like the one next door, like something out of a sitcom. It seemed impossible that anything bad could have ever happened here, and it seemed impossible that everyone's experience of it wouldn't be the same. All you needed to do was smile at your neighbour and wave.

'Weird comparison,' Orly said.

'What?'

'Treating TV as if it were the ultimate reality.'

'But those dreams are the blueprint for this place, not the other way around. It's the same idea as your resort.'

'My sanctuary.'

'Right,' I said, smiling. 'But every house here is an island. Neighbours are just a suggestion. Isn't that why you moved here?'

She reached across the parking brake and took my hand. 'Sure, yes. But how does that explain you?'

The way she was looking at me made me blush, and I pulled away. In front of this house, her touch made me nervous.

The lights in the Moradi house were on. No car was in the driveway, but he'd parked in the garage, at least when Ana and I were younger. It was innocent then. Ana and me hiding between the stools under the kitchen counter, listening to her mother chatter with her friends until we got bored and hid out in the garage and talked, sitting on the hood of his car. Sometimes it was still hot and clicking. Mrs. Moradi, Joyce, had a pair of velvet slippers she'd left out there, and I was scandalized that she let something so delicate and beautiful go to waste among the old boxes and oil stains, the decadence of her disregard. But she was the same with the sculptures she made at the art centre. After they'd been fired, she left them to the moss in the garden, but in the flower beds along the perimeter of the house there were no sculptures to be seen, no bending torsos, no abstract assemblages. I wondered if he and Joyce were still married, if he was at the art centre trying to get closer to her. Orly and I sat in the car for a while and saw no one. The lights could have been on a timer.

'Now what?' Orly asked.

I told her what had happened. I told her about it all.

'We could pee on his lawn,' she said.

I laughed and shook my head. 'What if he doesn't live here anymore?'

'Doesn't matter,' she said. 'It could be a symbolic gesture. Let it out and let it go.'

'What about the lawn?'

'One pee isn't going to ruin a lawn.'

I knew how wet the grass would be, the way the dark would feel, the sky and street. Being the only thing around that moved. I imagined squatting in it, trying not to get any on my shoes, my bare ass in view of the house. The windows of the house, eyes. I didn't want him to see me. I didn't want his eyes on me ever again. I wish I could say I thought he didn't deserve to look at me, but that's something Orly would have said. I was afraid of what his eyes would do to me. I had thought of all the ways I could get revenge on him. I had thought about it then, back in high school, and now. Everything from confronting him with Ana, hand-in-hand, to simply telling him to go fuck himself if I happened to run into him at the mall. I knew where he parked, so I could key his car. But when I actually thought about doing it, it left me limp. Nothing I did would make a difference. If I keyed his car, if I peed on his lawn, it would just be another way in which I was doing wrong. I'd be the one who seemed unhinged, and he'd come out of it looking like the reasonable one, the upstanding citizen, a family man. And if I told anyone else what happened in the parking lot, it would be my word against his – all I wanted to do was forget the whole story and let it sink into the past.

'You have every right to be angry,' Orly said.

'I'm not angry,' I said.

She didn't believe me. 'But what if you were?'

THE DIRECTOR'S HOUSE was far. Way past the freeway exit for my apartment in the city.

She had explained everything, but I didn't know what I was getting myself into. I looked at her and she smiled at me, and then all I was worried about was disappointing her.

Is this what she'd wanted all along: a colleague? It was exactly the kind of thing I got wrong: confusing lust, intimacy, and attention. *Colleague*. The word seemed absurd in this context. Sidekick. Assistant. Maybe *assistant* was better. Assistants didn't need to like the client, they just had to be supportive. I could do that. Would she take my hand again and hold me when it was over?

The dark hills rose around us on the freeway. Her hands were at ten and two on the steering wheel, her eyes darting between the mirrors and the road. I touched my blond wig and looked at hers. We were a striking pair. She trusted me to be here and that would have to be good enough.

I asked: 'How did he choose his coffin?'

'He's got a guy,' Orly said.

'A coffin guy?'

'I mean,' she shrugged. 'A guy. He's got a guy for all the stuff he wants to keep from his assistant.'

Orly said that after his Halloween party last year, when everyone else was asleep, she was watching the lights in the pirate maze Pete had built in his yard with set pieces his guy rented from the same prop house used by the studio who made the *Treasure Island* blockbuster, and she saw a coyote stepping lightly between the candy wrappers and red plastic cups. It stopped to look at her, ribs visible through its fur.

'Do you know why coyotes have to watch their backs?' she asked.

I shook my head.

'At first Coyote wanted death to be like sleep to spare us the grief, but Raven and the other scavengers were only thinking about feasting on fresh carcasses. They wanted death to be permanent, and made such a passionate case that Coyote gave in. Then Raven's daughter died and Raven begged Coyote to change his mind, but Coyote said what's done was done. Not a popular guy,' she said. 'But you learn a lot about people that way.'

She paused.

'They say that's why Coyote is always hungry. No one feels generously toward him because of the loss he caused.'

'Poor Coyote,' I said.

'Right? People don't understand mortality is also a gift.'

I thought about her story as we drove up the winding hill, passing one palatial home after the next. Maybe she was setting the tone. Everything about us felt gauzy and warm. I liked her loose way of telling stories, as though they were all true, and it didn't really matter which story you told because you got to choose what you carried with you. Orly turned onto a green residential street that twisted up a hill. With her story in my head and the lights playing on the window glass, I couldn't stop thinking how insubstantial these houses were. Houses like my parents' house, glass and steel, paper-thin walls, doors you could muscle open. Set in darkness and silence, how vulnerable we all are. The thought was exhilarating. Maybe this night would be transformative. Maybe it would be weird or boring. Whatever it would be, it would be with her and being with her felt urgent.

As soon as the Director opened the door, I was sure we knew each other from before, other than by reputation. Maybe we had gone to high school together. He laughed off the question, took our matching trench coats, and showed us through the living room, sunken with a cocktail bar. A wall of windows opened out onto a sprawling, manicured garden and a swimming pool. Everything was monochrome but the Technicolor movie posters. The walls were dappled with artificial shadows, their source a light covered with a gobo. In a bell jar on the table was a striped propeller hat, and then it clicked. I was about to tell the Director that I remembered where I knew him from, but Orly gripped my arm. She put her finger to her lips and shook her head. *Be cool.*

'The Director' was in fact little Petey Sandross. Everyone used to know him as Wendell, the sass-mouthed neighbour kid who wore that propeller hat in a popular family sitcom from the 1980s. His little-boy face – the famous cheesy grin, those grey eyes and jet-black hair belonging to the wise-beyond-his-years troublemaker – fought through the stubble and deep lines the sun and smoke and drink had given him. (Tabloid photos of him on the beach with women who towered over him, rumours of alcoholism, the cigarette that had seemed like a crutch in his teens now a fixture.) He was even smoking right then; his yellow teeth repulsive if he'd been anyone else. But this was Petey Sandross. He wouldn't be Petey Sandross, former child star, without that cigarette. I, we, everyone was invested in it. At least, until he'd dropped off the radar. I hadn't thought about him since I was a teen. But he was a person who didn't want to be reminded of his childhood stardom, even though it had afforded him all this. It was as though the early fame had stunted his growth and his very cells were clinging to those charmed years. However much he wanted to, he couldn't escape it, not even with a new career and a new name, not Petey but Peter J. Sandross, director.

Orly made a point of chatting with him about his last picture – another creature feature that might launch the career of another bombshell. The conversation was pointed. This is how we do it, she was suggesting.

'People must tell you all the time that you could be an actress,' Pete said to me. 'You've got *It*. Ever try it out?'

Orly's expression made me say, 'Try what out?'

'Acting.'

'Oh,' I said with practiced surprise. 'No, never. I leave that to the professionals.' I gestured to a scream queen on the wall. But there was that flutter. Maybe it wasn't a line.

'Don't be so modest,' Orly said. 'She'd be wonderful, Pete. Perfect against that creature…oh, what was it, again? I can never keep track of all your monsters.'

'The creature of Midnight Bay.'

He took his index finger and lifted up my chin. I gave him my best starlet eyes.

'I'm never wrong about these things.'

He studied me, moved my head left and then right, and grunted in agreement with his assessment.

'I turned Lola LaForce into a star, you know.'

I didn't.

'She wasn't getting anywhere as Elaine. Elaine Forcht. What is that: *forked*?' he said, taking a step back and a drag from his cigarette. The smoke streamed through his nostrils. In a singsong voice, he wondered: 'What will we call you?'

'Careful, darling,' Orly said. 'You're dropping names.'

'Whoopsadaisy,' he said, stubbing out his cigarette in a mirrored ashtray attached to a stuffed crow. The crow's head was bent, looking for its reflection beyond the ash.

On a credenza was a rubber chicken. He swept the prop into one drawer and opened another.

'You girls ever have trouble sleeping?' the Director asked.

'Oh, sure,' Orly said, earnest, afflicted.

'I've got just the thing,' he said. 'It comes in capsule form…'
We watched him take out one, two, three bullets, placing them on the white-veined marble.

He waved his hand over them like a magician. Orly put one hand to her chest in horror and with the other she reached for me.

'…and should be administered…'

Our attention was rapt; it pleased him.

He turned to face us, casually waving a gun, heavy and silver.

'With my handy contraption,' he said. It didn't look like a prop.

My dead body, he probably had a guy who could take care of that too. But something about the scenario felt familiar. I had seen it before, on an old TV show. Something by a master of horror. Hitchcock. The pastiche made me think the director was harmless. Interested in mimicry, not inventive enough to be diabolical.

Orly took my arm.

'You'll frighten the girl to death before we even get started. And I'll never be able to find you another blond at this time of night.'

Beyond the lawn where the pirate maze must have stood, the moon was a ravel in the carob trees. Orly and I made our way down the terraces. Fennel, nightshade, and sage. She said, 'Don't worry about noise. The neighbours can't hear a thing.'

A corona of light rose from behind the mountain ridges, all the lives I would not know. A burst of yelps and shrieks clattered in the canyon.

We came to a clearing: manicured lawn, rows of cutouts made to look like tombstones. There were path-lights, enough to create a glow. It might have been dust, but I liked to think the air was misty. It was cool down the hill. I could hear water flowing, but I wasn't sure from where. A broken sprinkler, perhaps. A filtration system mid-cycle, Jacuzzi water spilling into the pool. Waterfall.

And there was the coffin. Large and black. Silver handles glinting in the moonlight. Beside it an open grave. Had it been dug by his assistant? Did it ever get filled in?

The script we were working with said we were damsels cutting through a graveyard on our way to a party.

'Don't be afraid. Vampires aren't real,' Orly said to me, loud enough for someone inside the dark box to hear. We were supposed to let curiosity get the better of us and pause at the coffin. The lid swung open, narrowly missing my face, and the Director sat up straight, arms folded across his chest. Pale as chalk. We screamed. I screamed and screamed, and he chased us around the graveyard as we screamed. When he finally caught me – It was always going to be me who was caught first, before he was slain and buried – he pinned me against the tree and his pointy teeth pressed into my skin. The weight of Dr. Moradi, the hard shell of the car. The Director hinting he could make me a star. An open casket, a missing body. I lost it. I grabbed the prop crucifix and started stabbing him. I kept stabbing, even as he staggered away from me across the grass toward the gaping hole. I wasn't playing at fear anymore. I remember watching him fall into her arms, like it was in slow motion. How pathetic he was, his mouth open and surprised. The crucifix fell from my hand. My skin was wet, tears and sweat. I was very, very cold. Orly lay the Director's body on the grass. She shut his eyes and whispered something to him. I didn't want to come any closer. She waved me over to help her roll him into the hole. I stared at the man's body in his shallow grave, knowing he was not vanquished, knowing he would rise. I hated him, and to feel it all felt good. The space Orly had given me was a gift, too. I wanted to return to it.

When we were back in the car, after Pete had paid us, Orly asked me: 'Where did you go?'

AFTER THAT, ORLY'S HOUSE became the house of my imagination, awash with men.

They arrived with fantasies, most of which only made sense in action. This is what we were doing today: the client had fallen in a crowded nightclub and all the women were so busy grooving in their high heels they didn't notice. They thought he was the floor. Orly and I were all the women.

I struggled to keep my balance; she held my hands. I pressed into the balls of my feet, straining to stay on tiptoe for balance and bounce, shimmy, bounce. Each beat, we winded him. Each beat was a struggle to stand on his loose flesh, my soles stuttering across bone. The barrel of his chest. My ankle gave, and I slipped. The stiletto slid down his shoulder, and I found my footing on the hardwood floor. I could have broken his neck. Ended him. Ruined everything for her.

Blood rose from the abrasion and rolled down his white skin. He didn't seem to notice. Orly helped me back up, but I couldn't move. The give of his body, the give of his bones, as I struggled to be steady, careful to avoid his spine, but all I could see was a dead man, mouth ajar, fat red cheeks squished to the floor. He was so still. I couldn't keep dancing.

'You're bleeding,' I said.

One blue eye opened, and he shuddered when he whispered: 'Just. Keep. Going.'

Orly and I read their introductory letters, their questionnaires. She listened to them on the phone, noting the details of the woman they had in mind. What had Fumiko said? We accentuate the parts we find pleasing. We drew them with broad strokes.

The lipstick. The pencil skirt. The glasses. The suggestion of threat. The corseted waist and elongated leg. We focused on the parts they found pleasing, let pleasure render the perfect whole. Sometimes words led them only so far.

'I want to submit to you.'

'What does that mean to you?'

'I want you to be in control.'

'What would you like me to do?'

'Show me how inferior I am to you. Defile me.'

Orly needed specifics. When she couldn't push through, she'd hold their heads in her lap and rock them into a space of surrender, a gentle hypnosis, asking them to remember the first time they'd felt the desire to submit. To whom did they want to submit? What had that person made them do? What had they wanted the person to do? Often they'd wanted something that was impossible for them to say, but once they said it, everything was simple because we knew what to do. Sometimes they wanted to be watched while Orly worked on them, and I saw them go still, saw their breathing change. Their faces in ecstasy, a threshold crossed. Beyond fits of self-loathing or laughter. Beyond their pleas to Mommy or Daddy. Where did they trust her to take them when they allowed themselves to let go?

It felt good to be directed.

Told when to touch their extremities to see if they'd gone cold. To listen to the breath, to loosen the rope. They liked hearing her tell me why, where, and when. To hear her in control.

Here is where you land a blow. Avoid bones, the kidneys.

Take a large sip of wine, do not swallow. Purse your lips and make it stream onto his tongue. Fast. Before it gets too warm.

This one will ask for more but cannot take it. This whip makes a big sound, but not much of an impact.

Stroke the hair, but do not pull. (Hair plugs.)

Note the weak left knee.

This body bruises easily.

Watch.

I watched these men who came to her door and put their bodies in our care. They asked to be seen, and here they found their pleasure. In pleasure, they didn't have to be men anymore, only bodies in stillness and motion. Bodies of memory and yearning. Trusting her to sail them down currents of the unknown, and then to retrieve them, transformed.

We could have done anything to them. 'But we don't,' Orly said. The sense of responsibility was humbling. How tenderly I felt toward them. The way their skin changed colour when they strained against rope and the dark of their throats moved me deeply. Bodies I could break and people I could ruin, but who trusted me not to. Their trust made me attentive, and in our most brutal acts, their trust made me care. I wondered if this was what the men were feeling when they said they liked to watch me eat. It was a feeling like love.

I started to think I could face life in the city again. That I would be able to navigate it better and maybe even rise. I imagined how good I could be at making an appearance, using my powers not to be pleasing but to take control. I'd cultivate a new look. I'd drive to meetings in my father's car. I ran my hands around its tires, along the shelves in his closet, and I welcomed his smell. I couldn't find the keys, but I found his porn, and thought it sweet that he chose to look at women who had my mother's shape, sweeter even that he had such mild taste. There were handcuffs and nipple clamps, an enema kit in places that suggested they were no secret. I searched through drawers of permanent miscellany. Souvenir matches I'd collected after business dinners with other business families that had been dull but pleasant enough until the car ride home, the pen from a hotel we'd stayed at in Naples where he'd spent the last night of our vacation in his own room. I stuck the post-its he'd used to organize the books in his office to the windows of his car: Field Guides, Business, American West, and Fiction. I lined the grooves of the hood with trinkets. I leaned against the car with the garage door open, thinking of places we could have gone. In his baseball cap and university-logo shirt, I found my way down to the ledge and lay still in the sun and wind. Three planes overhead, Stearmen that had been flying this path for years. A man was paddling parallel to the coast. Pelicans flew low. His board slid into the sun, silhouette, shark, shard, swallowed by the light. I pressed my palms to the rock and shut my eyes. How long had he floated, had he floated past sunset, past sunset had there been another night of stars?

In these weeks, my blood was heavy with our erotic charge. Bliss dulled my mind, and I felt happy to be here in this charged system. With her, desire livened the days, and gave new life to the mundane. Nothing was itself alone, everything was a trigger for a fantasy, those of clients we had seen and my own. Lust was in play and in this free space, it grew in unexpected ways. When I came, it was because of her.

Orly ignored Piggy during these weeks we worked together. He continued to serve up his need alongside her, now our, morning coffee. I asked for cream, my colour was 15-1040. On his days of service, Piggy kept the couch cushions fluffed. He tidied up after us, ran Orly's errands and cooked dinner for three. Even then, she treated him coolly, as though he weren't really there. The things she made him watch, her focus on me, the warmth of our conversation, her casual touch. Of all we did in that house, Orly ignoring Piggy was the only thing that seemed cruel. He seemed to subsist on longing, and that didn't seem like enough. Once when I knew Piggy was looking, I slipped my foot from my shoe, baring my arch and heel. I thought she wouldn't notice, but Orly noticed everything.

ORLY AND I HAD SPENT the last hour puppy-training a new client who did everything he could to make us punish him even though he hadn't earned it, but Orly wasn't about to let us get pushed around. The naughty puppy had been a gift from my boyfriend, and I had to train it so it could stay with us in our dorm, undetected. Orly was the stern RA with a weak spot for puppies – and for female co-eds. Orly had him on a choke chain. He wouldn't stop straining. We were teaching him to sit. I had a bag of treats. He wanted them.

He charged at me, tearing the leash from her hands.

The hair on his shoulders, the strength of his back, his beast-liness apparent, the bulk of a man. His grabbing hands. I couldn't overpower him, so I stepped aside.

He skidded across the floor and knocked into her large oak chair. That's when he snapped. He planted his hands on the seat of the chair, hoisted himself onto two feet, turned to us and said: 'I want my treats.'

'That's not how it works. Should we pause and go over what we discussed on the phone?'

'You can dress up what you do all you like, but the truth is you're a whore, and I paid for you.' He grabbed Orly's wrist, and she clenched the wooden paddle more tightly. 'So reward me, whore.'

Orly jerked her hand free. She didn't even flinch, but what flickered across her face made something crack inside me. I pictured Orly in a black bob that contrasted with her lunar skin, waist cinched to a wisp. Orly, wreathed in smoke, a long cigarette holder in her gloved hands. Orly bending a stingray cane. Orly in a candy-pink latex dress, breasts pushed up to her chin. And then this Orly, swimming in her leggings and my dad's university T, which she'd knotted above her belly button. Clothing not worn but put on. Her persona shaped by the men against whom she was braced. She could speak to me of goddesses – of Inanna who stole from her father the wisdom that laid the foundation of our first great civilization, point to her vulva and command a man to kneel before her fearsome power – but what we created in her space fell apart if not everyone was playing. We might play at power, exploring roles not yet available to us outside these four walls, but for the space to be sacral, it had to be held sacred by us all.

Orly flicked on the overhead light and opened the door, shouting into the house for Piggy, except she used his Christian name, those blunt syllables a warning, which sent the man scurrying into the bathroom to fetch his everyday clothes. 'Crazy bitches,' he hissed when he emerged, swatting Piggy away. The man was much bigger than Piggy, who in his khakis and button-down shirt looked harmless, but Piggy used persuasion, not force. I listened to their footsteps on the stairs, to the front door open and close. Orly was typing on her phone. She smirked and said, 'He's done for,' and showed me a post she had left on a forum, but I saw her hands were shaking. I reached for her, but Orly didn't want to be touched. Still I didn't want to leave her alone. A sharp smell came from the bathroom. There was a puddle on the floor.

Piggy came back to say he had watched him drive away, the man was gone. Then he smelled it too. As Piggy walked into the bathroom, Orly didn't even look up from her phone when she said: 'This isn't your mess.'

He stopped in the doorway and she pushed past him, unspooling the toilet paper and balling it up in her hands. 'It's not for you.'

I couldn't move. As Piggy led me out of the room, I was sure I heard her crying. My lover is crying, I thought. I had thought she was invincible, which meant I hadn't really been thinking about her at all. And now she didn't want me, us, near her. Of course not. I heard my heart inside her beating. *I'd forgotten about you.*

'It'll blow over,' he said. 'We need to give her some space. What's left on your to-do list?'

I didn't feel fit for anything, but my mind seized the idea of a task, and it was as though an automated process was set in motion. Doing the tasks she'd set out for me was a way to stay close to her. It would do for now. I clung to Piggy's words. It would blow over.

'I still have to take care of the mail,' I said.

We took storage boxes from the bookshelf, which were filled with envelopes, photos of her, plastic bags, as well as used tissues, T-shirts, briefs, thongs, and sweaty socks. All to be packaged and sent off. I had printed the mailing labels the day before and put them in a plastic sleeve with a spreadsheet detailing what was to go where. We set up a production line on the table.

I sealed a pair of worn panties in a plastic bag, put the bag in a plain white envelope. A note on top, written by Orly and sealed with a kiss. I handed the package to Piggy, which he placed in a padded envelope and stuck the mailing label on. I marked the first item on the spreadsheet as having been processed. From my hands to Piggy's hands to the postman's hands, every pair of hands handling it until it landed in a po box in Arizona. What would be left of us when it arrived?

We took Piggy's boxy, brown car to the post office. He drove. The sun was harsh, and inside the car the hot air was thick with new-car-smell air freshener. I rolled the window down. Exhaust and salt cut through the heat.

'Is this because I showed you my feet?'

'No. She never minds when her girls play with me.'

Girls. Play. I knew I wasn't the first to assist with her work, but I didn't like to think of myself as 'girls.' It felt like sitting in a waiting room before an audition. A roomful of girls each one like the other, each of us replaceable.

'All I've ever wanted in life was for a woman to let me have access to her feet, you understand. Until you flashed me…' He inhaled deeply. 'I was scared. Orly really likes you, and I didn't know where that'd leave me.'

'Where does it leave you?'

He gave me a panicked look. 'What if she gets bored of me?' I thought he was going to cry.

I put my hand on his shoulder, and he shrugged it off. 'You don't understand,' he said.

And so I let him be. I leaned back in my seat and into the dark mood in the car. Orly, a fickle figure looming large, and the two of us reading her signs, wanting to do nothing but please her and still getting it wrong. I had gotten lost in a fantasy of Orly, Orly my lover, my healer, my authority figure. In my fog of lust and sorrow, in all my need, I hadn't seen her. I hadn't given her the space she had given me to unfold, to get to know her. And if I did… The thought felt like falling.

The post office sat atop a hill overlooking the harbour. Cruise ships were lingering out in the water. The parking was impossible. We found a spot around the corner and a young punk, shaky on his legs and hanging with his friends, started barking at Piggy about what he was hiding under his shirt. I caught a glimpse of red rope knotted around his neck and chest, the lines it made under his clothes. He caught me looking, and buttoned up his shirt so the strip of chest no longer showed.

When I went home that day, I didn't go to the garage. I sat with my mother in her room. I asked her what she needed. I cleared away her dirty dishes and orange peels. I brought her dinner and then breakfast the next day, tea and fruit because the volume of casserole I'd heated up the night before seemed to overwhelm her. I visited the mailbox and tugged the mass of envelopes free. I set up automated payments for the bills. I encouraged her to wash. I washed her clothes and bedding. I set traps for ants seeking respite from the heat. Whether or not she was awake, whether or not she was kind, I wanted her to know I would not be like my father. I would not abandon her.

PIGGY REMEMBERED HIS early days with Orly.

The night they met in the strip club, she'd seen inside him like no one else had. She understood him, and this alone would have been enough to secure his devotion. But after that came the hard work: learning about each other, setting boundaries so they knew where her work and his service ended and their friendship began. But there was a learning curve: what was good pain, what did compassionate cruelty look like, how would they manage their desires between them and with the outside world? He recalled her hunger for pain. In her first year working with him, she'd been quick to strike, giving no thought to her poison, what it took out of her, or how her wild pain affected him. To balance herself out, she craved a pain equally wild and unchecked. She found people who would hurt her. Cruelty for cruelty, pain for pain. But it was unsustainable: to be filled only to be drained.

One day she asked him if there was anything more she could do. He considered the cycle they were in, and wrote this letter:

For much of my life, I wanted nothing more than to be intimate with God, but I found no model for myself in the Church. I briefly considered joining the priesthood, just to have a sanctioned way to mortify my flesh. I was already largely celibate. I didn't identify as a virgin – the word contained too much hope for a future I knew would not be mine. I'd listened to other boys boast about their conquests, imagined or real. I understood my interests were abnormal, I kept my mouth shut or repeated what they had said. I cut off this dialogue with myself and when I did dare to fantasize about what I wanted, it involved a punishment because there was no way I could seek pleasure for pleasure's sake. Each orgasm confirmed what I thought to be true: I was a freak. I lost my self-respect. I dreamed of violence.

I did not know where God was in all of this. If I had forsaken him. Periods of celibacy in adulthood did not grant me a return. For in those years – and I was a late-bloomer, losing my virginity long after everyone else had, to a woman who was sure I was a good Christian man – not a day went by that I could keep my fantasies at bay. I wanted. I did not allow myself to want. But what if this force was part of God? It was stronger than my will, it overtook prayer and confession.

I did what I knew how to do. I turned my focus to worship. I imagined a woman with a heart large enough to contain me. I focused my desires on her. I collected every scrap of her I could find. I adapted a psalm and it became my prayer: 'One thing I ask of Woman, this only do I seek: that I may dwell in the house of Woman all the days of my life, to gaze on the beauty of Woman and to seek Her in Her temple.' I wished to serve a Goddess who takes genuine sadistic pleasure in my submission to Her Will. I wanted to be in a cage of lust, to be taunted with the key that could release me. I wanted Her to render me helpless. Poke and prod. Restrain me. Penetrate me. (But no electro-play or needles.) I wished to be humbled in the presence of Her Superior Sex. It is the power of Her Sex after all that makes the world turn; it drives us to industry and makes servants of men like me. Men who know their rightful place is at her feet, nose to ground and lips to the dust.

I showed my love for Her through ritual and obedience, caring not if my love was returned. I was sure that an intimate connection would appear to me should I seek it. And then You appeared, and the glory of You was greater than what I'd known of love.

He had watched her read the letter. She set it aside. After that, she no longer let herself be beat black and blue only to turn the same rod on him. She let his words sink in. She let herself be exalted. He found a new vitality. He lost eight pounds and regained them in muscle. Gone were the bags under his eyes. He felt bold and returned to his career. And he found new ways to delight her: taking classes that ranged from boot-blacking to the culinary arts. He learned to braid hair. Tenderness tempered cruelty, patience mixed with pain. Whenever they met, there was an exchange. There was a calibration.

IT WAS A REGULARLY scheduled session, but everything I had been doing for Orly was done. The curtains were drawn, the room was cool. The room with its dark walls and strange angular furniture seemed liquid in the glow of the candles Piggy was lighting.

When I joined him and Orly in the sanctuary, I noticed a change. Piggy wasn't asserting himself, and he was focused on his tasks. Orly waved a burning smudge stick in my direction. She said: 'I thought we could clear out the space. Reset the energy.' There was something conspiratorial about them, playful.

'OK,' I said, but I was nervous. I didn't understand who the room was being prepared for. Orly's other clients existed only in these confines – it was part of what I enjoyed about engaging with their desire. It didn't follow me into the real world. If she asked me to play with Piggy, I'm not sure that I could. I'd be self-conscious, or perhaps his devotion to Orly, the claim he had on her, might manifest in an unpleasant way. But I wanted Orly to have her ordered world. The sage smoke made me feel heavy and slow.

The leather bench was oiled, the wooden floor waxed, and the paddle, razor strop, and flogger laid out on a cloth on the table. I grabbed the flogger as one would a ponytail and brought it to my nose, its leather fresh and soft. 'Will we use all of these?' I asked.

'If you want,' Orly said. 'They're for you.'

'It was Piggy's idea,' she added, and he smiled at me, a smile that ceded the space. It was a generous act, and I was grateful to him. He finished lighting the candles and left us alone. Orly stood close to me and ran her hands over my neck, down my shoulders and arms. 'He thought you maybe needed a little special attention.' She put her hand to my heart. 'A release.'

I nodded. I wanted to know where she would take me. I put the flogger aside and asked for her hand because I wanted nothing between us but skin.

I bent over the bench, as she instructed.

Orly said: 'Repeat after me.'

She spoke slowly to me. Six simple rhythmic lines. A melody of maidens and the sea. Repeating after her, the words became my own. She smoothed her hands over my bottom. I felt it warm. When I found my rhythm, she began to spank me. Fluttering smacks and some that stung, running her fingers down my parting line, spine and cunt. The lines began to break, and my words fell to pieces, and when I faltered, she said, 'Begin again.' Each syllable a blow, harder with each mistake.

Hold still, she said, *hold still. Breathe through it. Begin again.* I held still. I focused on my breath. I listened to the words and I repeated them until I knew them by heart. I said them through pain, I said them with pain, I said them in pain. I let the pain remake me. The words became a chant. A chant became sound, sound rode the edge of silence and dropped into the waves. A blue drum, swirling silver bodies in the ocean, among which I was one, circling the light. And in this light I saw my father. In the light, we spoke.

When I came to, my skin stung with tears, my mouth was salty and the air was thick with smoke. My body wet and hot but cooling. I felt raw and slack, and an extraordinary sense of calm, like the days I'd wake up with a hangover that didn't hurt but reminded me to be soft with myself, the giddiness of being new to the world. Orly covered me with a thin robe, stroked my back until I remembered my feet and she helped me find them. Piggy had drawn me a bath and brought me something to drink. I sank into the tub and lay in the luxury of their care. Loss, I thought, did not have to be a void of grief and pain, it could also be an encounter: there I would find him, reaching through the deep, rising on the altar of the tides. I thought about how a tide has no beginning or end, it is a single wave pinwheeling around the ocean, at its centre a point of stillness, a place of no tide. I laid my hands where hers had been. This wasn't pain I had endured, it was pain to which I listened. As I dried myself off, I saw in the mirror livid marks were rising to the surface, rising to fade.

THE SEATS IN PIGGY'S CAR were itchy. I couldn't seem to find a comfortable spot. I tugged at my skirt, which wasn't particularly short but rode halfway up my thighs when I sat down. My legs were bare, and the upholstery prickled. Every time I moved, my bottom ached. This discomfort I enjoyed. I liked feeling her with me, and I was looking forward to tonight. I was also looking forward to seeing my car again. I missed my wheels, but I didn't really miss my apartment. Maybe it was time to give it up.

Piggy took his eyes off the road, looked at me squirming and laughed. 'It's the best part,' he said. 'Healing. It reminds me that my body works and everything is as it should be. I'd get myself some arnica and Epsom salt. To have handy.'

'I don't want to heal any faster,' I said.

'I know.'

'What about you?'

'It's not about me.'

I felt a rush through my thighs. Possibility, but also sadness. I didn't want my satisfaction to be at his expense.

Bach came on the radio.

He said: 'I've always wanted to hear this piece live.'

'I have,' I said. 'In Munich. The conductor took a lot of liberties, and my mom was not into it at all. She stood up right there in the concert hall, said *pfui* so everyone, even the orchestra, could hear, and then she left. My dad said it was part of her Alpine temperament. My dad and I, we followed her. We didn't know what else to do.'

'She didn't get what she came for. You know how that can go.' He gave me a sideways look, and I laughed not because it was funny but in recognition of how quickly people can turn, and how I had to get better at reading the signs. 'I thought we were going to a party,' I said.

'You're right. Should we keep talking about music? Is that what you talk about when you go out?'

'I have no idea what I talk about. Not music. People find other things interesting about me. So I stopped trying.'

When he pulled up at my apartment building, I almost didn't recognize it. He parked behind my car. The jacaranda in front of the building was no longer in bloom, but my car was covered in its sap.

'Don't dilly dally,' Piggy said. 'I gotta have someone to commiserate with over the music.'

'What do they play?' I said.

'Classic rock. Even with all the beautiful women there, it makes it so hard to get in the mood.'

I brushed dried flowers off my car, but some of the petals stuck. I'd have to stop by the gas station and give the windows a scrub. I'd wash it when I got back home. I ran my hand along the line of the trunk and the doors. The car chirped when I unlocked it. I like to think it was happy to see me. As I fiddled with the windshield wipers and spray, trying to clear a window so I could have a little visibility, I got a text. I was hoping it was Orly. She was meeting us there. She and one of her regulars were going out for dinner before the doors opened. He'd paid a premium. In the run-up to a foot party, she was in high demand. She'd been receiving text messages all week. 'Some heat we're having today,' a message from one of the men who'd scheduled a session during the party had read. 'I'm thinking about your sweaty feet squishing in those sneakers.'

'Foot guys are adorable,' Orly had said. 'You'll have fun. If you get into it, you can make way more than rent money in one night.' She made it sound easy – like what we were already doing, and I loved being with her. Maybe we could have our own cottage industry down the by the sea. A self-sufficient bubble, complete in and of itself, where everyone was happy. I could help shoot and edit her videos. I could find other ways to be useful and to generate new streams of income. Orly and me, and sometimes Piggy.

But it wasn't Orly sending me messages. It was Van.

'Hey,' it read. 'You around?'

I counted to ten before I responded. The gall, I thought. But something in me felt entitled. I wanted to see what he had to offer.

VAN SAID HE HAD TAKEN over a rooftop at a hotel to send off his star before he headed out on a global press tour. He'd said he was sorry about our date and wanted to make it up to me, plus he'd introduce me to some people who were good to know. Backlit palms and bamboo cast stark shadows. Guests crowded around a swimming pool, its light turning their skin blue. Everything had a soft pulse to it, the music, the headlights sliding down the boulevard, a hazy twinkle in the hills. Waiters with wide smiles balanced trays of drinks and canapés. People weren't really touching the food.

A magician I knew was dazzling two women in tight dresses with a trick that left them each with an X on their palm. I watched him perform the trick a second time, the one girl keeping a close eye on his every move, delighted when her friend opened her clenched fist and a new X had appeared in black marker. I wondered if he'd seen Van.

'Van?' The magician said he didn't know him. A friend had texted him about the party, and he'd walked up after his act at the Magic Castle. 'Didn't even have to move my car,' he said. He touched my waist, glanced at the shoes I'd borrowed from Orly, and bit his lip.

She'd said shoes tell you how they want to be used, and I liked that this pair was speaking to the magician. Watching him respond to them felt like being let in on a secret. I wondered if the women he was performing for noticed. But I hadn't worn these shoes for him or this party. I didn't want to make Piggy wait too long.

It was crowded, and I wandered around looking in corners and cabanas. I didn't see anyone I knew and no one I asked knew

Van. There was something about the way one of the men was telling a story to a group gathered around a fire pit, how he commanded their attention, that made me think these might be Van's people.

They were laughing at a man with a bushy but tidy beard doing a Cockney accent. Every once in a while he fidgeted with his trucker hat and I caught a glimpse of his shiny bald head. His T-shirt said '~~degeneration~~ REGENERATION' and his arms were sculpted, an odd contrast to his soft gut. I perched on the arm of a rattan sofa to take the weight off my feet. The shoes were wearing me out.

'And I haven't even got to the good part yet. Lola and Chase, they're supposed to be having *that moment…*' He winked at me. It was a sweet move. I decided to stay. I didn't even feel jealous hearing the name 'Lola.' 'So they're walking through the desert, all strapped into their gear. It's a million degrees. They've been shooting for hours. Everyone wants to go home. We'd already lost the morning to a dust storm. And suddenly Chase goes to Lola: *Don't move a muscle*. And those two with their chemistry – I mean look at his fucking baby blues, who wouldn't do whatever he says – '

He gestured into the group. I scanned the benches, the people leaning against the railing. There was Chase, set against a backdrop of shimmering night.

'… Lola freezes. Good girl, right?' he said, nodding, encouraging us all to agree. 'She's mid-step. Her heel is down but the toe of her boot is hovering above the ground…' He demonstrated. 'Chase goes: *When I say 'now' take one big slow step backward.* He's pulling his machete out.' The bearded man crouched low and mimed pulling out a machete. The fire cast strange shadows on his face. The crowd was in his thrall.

'And with the tip of his knife…' He showed us all how big the knife was. '…he flings a friggin' *baby rattlesnake* out of her path. She'd been standing on its tail. Do you understand: Its. Tail. And saves her life. I'm watching the director, waiting for him to cut – I'm Chase's assistant, but he's also my buddy, and I'm freaking out here – but he keeps the camera rolling, and I don't know where to look. At Lola and Chase, or at the monitor, because those two: cinema gold. You're gonna shit when you see it.' He paused to wink at his friend and then turned back to the crowd. The woman standing next to Chase put her hand on his chest, stood on tiptoe and whispered in his ear. He smiled.

'And this guy is so humble. Ever since we were kids. When I say: Buddy! You saved her life! He goes: I grew up in San Diego, man. We got snakes.'

The bearded man raised his glass, 'I'm so proud of you. Here's to my best friend.'

Those who had glasses raised them expectantly. But where Chase had been was now just railing. Something shifted in the group. The pause was a beat too long. Chase's childhood friend didn't know how to save himself from the silence. The people at edge of the group walked away, and then a handful of us were left sitting on the sofas. Only then did I see that painted on the side of a tall building was Chase Cardoso's face one hundred and fifty feet tall. Fuckin' Van, I thought. The guy knew how to work it without making it look like work at all. Across from it on the building's twin was Lola. Chase was handsome like you'd expect him to be, but nothing special, except that he was next to a woman like Lola. Everything about her was otherworldly. I'd never seen her image so large. I struggled to see our likeness. Of course, she was blond now and that can make all the difference. Maybe it was the scale.

Chase's childhood friend tried to save himself by directing his toast at the painted movie ad, raised his bottle of beer in the air, and said, 'To Chase,' but he'd lost it. I thought of the Seven

Sisters again. Orion had seen them frolicking on earth and was captivated by their beauty, these companions of Artemis, and their beauty drove him mad. He had to possess it. After years of being chased and begging for Zeus to help them, Zeus turned the Sisters into stars. But this didn't save them from the hunter. He set Orion in the sky, too, where he would forever be in hot pursuit. Even Artemis, who crosses the sky in her chariot and gets in Orion's way at regular intervals, cannot end their mad dash. What a cruel thing to turn the Sisters into stars, I thought. Reversing their humanity. However far they had come, they were but stardust again, back at square one. I left.

A TEXT CAME IN from Van: 'Did I miss you?'
    And later: 'Must have missed you.'
    Then nothing.

I TOOK OFF MY SHOES in the elevator and walked through the hotel lobby and waited for the valet to fetch my car. It was well past eleven. Piggy said he was getting there for ten. I assumed Orly and her client would be finished with dinner and already inside. The drive wasn't far, but the traffic was heavier than I excepted, and I seemed to hit every red light. I drove deep into the city, past the produce market, past the homeless camps. I thought I recognized party spaces where I had seen fire-spinners and art shows, places I'd spent the tail end of endless nights with too much of everything and too little sleep, but it was still unfamiliar territory. Not a light was on in the warehouses, their windows pocked, the pavement outside buckled. The night was sweet and sharp with fermented fruit and urine. A security guard was watching the alley where Orly said I should park.

I walked up a shaky metal staircase and knocked on the door. Peering through a heavy curtain was a man with a greasy ducktail, scowling as he looked me up and down. He nodded and let me in, locking the door behind me. On his folding table was a newspaper, a cash box, a binder, and a half-eaten granola bar.

He found my name on the guest list: 'Orly always brings in the prettiest ones. You're not as.' He gestured around his face. 'Done up. It's nice to see a natural beauty.' Pointing his pen at me, he said, 'Don't you tell anyone I said so.'

He led me down a long hallway lined with doors. It was oddly silent. I couldn't tell where the party was.

'No nudity. No genital touching. No hand jobs, no blow jobs. Nada. Got it? No cum. Don't take less than twenty bucks every ten minutes, otherwise the other ladies'll get mad.' He rapped on one of the doors, and, while opening it, said, 'Just keeping you honest' to a couple in a bare black-lit chamber. The man was unusually still, the woman looked up. The word 'trance' came to mind, and I remembered my point of stillness.

'Gotta keep the doors open,' he told me.

'OK.'

He repeated himself, articulating each word. 'The doors *gotta* stay open.'

I nodded, but he just looked at me. I wasn't sure what he wanted. 'You've made yourself crystal clear,' I assured him.

'OK,' he said. 'All I'm doing is keeping everything on the level. It's a good party. They're an easy hire.'

He showed me where the lockers were, and I put away my bag and freshened up. I hadn't been in a locker room like that since high school. Metal and concrete. Communal showers. I worried that the entranced couple and I were among the first to arrive. I hoped the room the party was in wouldn't be as cold.

The double doors at the end of the corridor opened on to a vast warehouse. It wasn't empty, but it wasn't full. Classic rock was blaring from the speakers, like Piggy had said, and something about the space – the folding tables, fairy lights, and smoke machine – reminded me of prom. A potluck buffet was spread across a set of white plastic tables. There was potato salad and casserole. On a table off to the side were bags of cotton balls and bottles of witch hazel. A woman in a blue latex dress was spinning around the pole on the stage. Men gazed up at her. Sofa groups were scattered around the room, arranged so you couldn't see what was going on, only whether or not they were occupied.

Women in club wear, business suits, shift dresses, little black dresses, burlesque dancers' outfits were perched on stools along the bar. Thigh-high boots. Peep toes. Toe cleavage. In a club chair near the bar, a woman in a pink peignoir and shoes that could not bear any weight was being waited on by three men. One rubbed her shoulders, the other was sliding the stiletto heel into his mouth. He gagged. The third held a tray with her drink and looked straight ahead.

I asked the woman next to me if she knew Piggy and she responded, 'Which one?'

I ordered a double shot of vodka and drank it in one go. It hadn't occurred to me that I might have to be in the mood to do this work. I'd never had to get in the mood with Orly. I couldn't see her or Piggy, and no one seemed to want to talk. When I tried to strike up a conversation with the other women, I could feel them looking over my shoulder. I had finally gotten some traction with a woman, who was telling me about her problems with cheap lingerie. I wouldn't say she was friendly. She was factual, like a stranger at a gas station telling you where you took a wrong turn. And without excusing herself, she walked straight up to a man behind me, and they disappeared into one of the dark rooms.

The vodka had settled me a bit, made me think 'not being in the mood' was nerves and maybe the music.

I caught a man in a tan leisure suit looking at my shoes, and smiled because I seemed to have startled him. Taking my cue from the other women, I approached him. Not too fast. I wanted him to get a good look. The veins across the top of my feet were thick with the strain of wearing high heels. It had been a mistake to take them off. My feet felt swollen when I'd put them back on. He seemed as nervous as I was.

I said hello.

'What made you come over?' he asked. Wringing his hands, he didn't seem to know where to look: my feet, my face, the room.

'I thought we might have something in common.'

'Is this your first time, too?'

'It is,' I said.

'Oh good. I'm not sure what to do. There are so many beautiful ladies. And you're all *here*. I didn't know what to expect.'

'Do you want to figure it out together?'

We found an unoccupied sofa group. Purple velvet with a gold trim far away from the banquet tables and the bar.

'Sumptuous,' he said. I agreed, to be polite.

'Let's start with ten minutes and see how it goes,' I said, taking a seat on the sofa. Using the information the doorman had given me made me feel a little more in control. The man immediately kneeled on the floor, hovered his face over my shoes.

'Nice shoes. Expensive. Did you buy these yourself?'

'Of course,' I said. 'A girl can treat herself, can't she?'

He looked up at me: 'Woman. A woman can treat herself.'

I said nothing, and tried to look pleased. Neither word felt like it applied to me.

'They're nice shoes. Really nice. If you were mine, I'd buy you these shoes in every colour.'

'I'd like that.'

He was quivering. He took off his jacket, folded it neatly and placed it on the ottoman. His cologne hung in the air. I tried to be subtle about checking my watch. Barely two minutes had passed.

'May I?'

'Please.'

He traced the edges of my shoes and stuck his finger in the peep-toe.

'You've been running around in these all night,' he said. He gripped my feet and squeezed them together.

'I was at another party.'

'What kind of a party?'

'A Hollywood party.'

'I knew it. I thought you might be an actress, or a model.'

He took off my right shoe and pressed his nose to my sole. 'You were barefoot.'

I laughed at his powers of detection, and embellished: 'Yes. I even drove here without shoes on. I like how the pedals feel.'

He moaned and licked my foot from heel to toe. He fell into a rhythm. He knew exactly what he wanted to do. He used his tongue. He used his nose. He massaged my feet and calves, finding pressure points and releasing every tension in me. All the while muttering about how lucky he was to have found a woman like me, a fine young lady. A woman who liked to have her feet touched. Who let him do it. A successful actress with good style, a natural model beauty. The kind of woman he could introduce to his mother. I started getting into it, the fantasy that I was a perfect woman offering what no other woman could. I felt special, like when I'd shown off my feet to Piggy. Like some sort of saviour.

'Oh,' he said. 'Oh, oh. I could fall for you. You're a woman I could marry.'

He pressed my soles to his chest, which shuddered as he sighed.

'I could fall in love with you,' he muttered and sounded so sincere that for a second I thought I could, too.

He put my shoes back on my feet. They didn't feel swollen at all.

Then he stood up, handed me a twenty, said thank you and walked away.

Exactly ten minutes had passed.

His saliva had made my feet sticky and I didn't like the way it felt between my toes.

I was sitting at one of the round tables near the buffet, thinking about my car and how I wanted to go home, when Piggy appeared.

He gave me a warm hug and said, 'Have you been having a good time?'

'Yes,' I lied. I didn't want to ruin his party. 'Have you seen Orly?'

'No, but she's somewhere.'

'You were right about the music.'

He looked around to make sure no one had heard me and then gave me a look that said, 'I told you so.'

'The potluck's a nice touch,' I said.

'It's a good bunch of people.'

'Could I help with the mood?' I asked, mostly as a way to pass the time. And maybe it would feel different with Piggy, someone with whom I had a connection.

He looked at Orly's shoes and then in the direction of the man in the leisure suit.

'You've already been with him?'

'Yes.'

'Then no thanks. Nothing against your lovely… I'm a little…'

'I get it.'

'No offence.'

'It's fine.'

'It's why I get here early.'

'Really, I'm OK.'

He could tell I wasn't really.

'How about I clean them for you?'

Piggy returned with a bottle of witch hazel and sat in a chair across from me, my foot resting on his jeans. He swabbed my foot with damp cotton balls, and when he slipped my shoes back on, the skin squeaked against the leather.

And that's when I saw Orly.

Orly issued a command I'd never heard, but Piggy knew what

it meant. He looked surprised. He had been expecting her, but not this. As soon as the backs of his hands were resting on his knees, you could see everything in the room had fallen away for him but her. With the point of her cane, she prodded him and he crawled across the floor and up the steps to the stage. I moved to the edge of the platform, where a small crowd had gathered. She had him stand at the edge of the stage, facing us. They were on full display, but something about them was private. I'd never seen her play with such intensity. She took her time. She teased him through his clothes. Then she spoke into his ear. He looked frightened, but nodded and undressed slowly, bashfully, stopping at his black leather thong. Everyone was looking. Then she took out his rope, silky and red. I'd glimpsed it under his shirt, but I hadn't seen how the harness was constructed before. Piggy always hid his body from me. She laid out a pad for his knees and had him kneel. The rope draped around his neck and slid across his chest, knots and strands crossing his torso and wrapping around his thighs and between his legs. Her hands never touched his skin. We could see the hairs on his arm rise, and then she took out the clippers. Through the din of drums and guitars, they buzzed. Piggy was trembling.

Orly stood beside him and lifted his chin. Again, she spoke to him, but we couldn't hear. They looked at each other for a long while. A few people went back to the buffet and bar, tired of the spectacle or wanting one of their own. With one hand, she took him by the chin, clasping him along the jaw. She hooked her thumb over the bottom row of his teeth. The clippers on her other hand, she began to shave his head. Locks of dark hair fell on shoulders, dusted his chest and drifted to the ground, landing on his feet. When she was finished she wiped him clean and guided him up to his feet. He seemed unsteady, eyes locked to hers. He fell into her arms.

Her words were a bridge revealing the space between them. No one but Piggy could hear Orly say: *I decide if and when I use you. Are we clear?*

We're clear.

When Orly and Piggy left the stage, the room began to move again. Piggy sat at one of the round tables, wearing only his harness, sneakers, and thong. He was getting used to being in his skin. He got up and went to the buffet, poured a glass of water and helped himself to a strawberry from the fruit plate. When he touched his shaven head, he looked happy. I saw the way people looked at him now. They knew to whom he belonged. She had left her mark, and he was free to roam. A woman came over to speak with him, they hugged, and found a space where they could be alone.

MOTHER

THE NEXT DAY, I searched the house for my mother. She wasn't in her bedroom or in the yard. I feared the worst, but then thought that my mother was too proud to negate her own creation. The last place I looked was in the garage. When I saw her sitting there, in Dad's Karmann Ghia, I wanted to throw my arms around the hood of the car.

She rolled down the driver's side window and offered me a Beer Nut. There was about half of the packet left. The sweet spot. Enough sugared and salted husks had fallen off so the bag was half-full of flavored dust that you could scoop up along with a peanut. I dug my fingers in and stuck them in my mouth, but then I couldn't chew or swallow. She took my hand.

'Come sit,' she said, reaching across the seats to open the passenger door.

The smell inside. Stale and intimate. Years of crumbs, breath, sweat, dust, and air-fresheners. We added to it our sorrow. Our noses started running and we laughed when we saw what the other was using as a tissue: the collar of my shirt, the back of her hand.

I reached into his seat pocket and felt around for his stash of take-out napkins. I touched his *Thomas Guide* map, plastic cutlery, and driving gloves. Reading glasses, half-drunk bottles of water. A comb. Mints. The kind of mess that makes you say you live in your car. A casual collection of everyday items that could only have come from him.

'Where did he keep the key?'

'One of the canisters of tennis balls had a false bottom. I knew we had a key rock and a fake can of soup, but I didn't know about the tennis balls. You know how he was when we misplaced our keys.'

We sat in silence for a while.

My mother glanced at me and said: 'The art centre called.'

I couldn't read her tone.

'They said you never picked up your cheque.'

Silence.

'I didn't know you were working.'

'I quit.'

She frowned.

'Dr. Moradi was in my class.'

No one could look as dignified in anger as my mother.

'I don't know how Joyce can stand to be with that man. His own daughter won't even speak to him anymore.'

'Ana won't?'

She nodded.

I let it sink in.

I said: 'But you didn't leave Dad either. Even though you wanted to end it, both of you, didn't you?'

'Since your father…'

'Drowned.'

'Yes,' she said and reached across the gear shift to take my hand. Her nails were shell pink, and where they'd grown out were pale, bare crescents. Her cuticles were dry and the polish chipped. 'I keep thinking about how I ended up here. One day, I'm managing the Rotterdam office, the next I'm at the town hall with my co-worker getting married,' my mother said. 'Even then I was sure it was all a mistake. He thought this…'

She touched my arm as one does in conversation, as I did and do. It reminded me of other times when it was easier to smile: a week into a two-week vacation when Dad finally relaxed, or when she'd reach over and touch my arm to tell me everything was under control as she speeded up before the slope where the landslide had lifted the earth under the road. If she hit the incline just right, the car would catch air.

'...was me coming on to him. I thought his eagerness was foolish at first. Boyish. I was a woman paying attention to him. But we were at that age and both wanted children, and when he talked about California...well. Your father loved me. I had no idea why, but he was there, offering himself to me, so sure of us from the start. Who was I to say no? He made me laugh, he adored me, and we wanted the same things, at least for a while. He was – '

' – an excellent salesman?'

The words made her flinch.

She continued: 'Twenty-six years is a long time for anyone to be in the wrong place.'

'Why didn't you leave?'

'And be a divorcée here?' she scoffed and seemed to detach from the conversation, no longer speaking to me, but announcing a general truth. Her tone of voice made me sad. 'And have you shuttling between him in our home and me in whatever *condo* the alimony would buy me? No thank you. I could never have done that to you.'

Why she wouldn't allow herself to imagine divorce as a fresh start, I don't know, and if I asked, there was a risk it would end with us screaming. It was her attitude, I realized, that provoked me. It hurt to hear that she had locked herself into an idea of being. I wanted to wrestle her away from her preconceptions. But she didn't want me to come up with solutions. I think she just wanted me to be there to witness her wounds. I could do that.

'It must have been tough,' I said.

My mother brought my hand to her lips, then pressed it to her chest, rising and falling with her breath, her heart beating steady below.

We passed the bag of peanuts between us, and when they were all gone, she took my fingers in her hands and looked at my nails: 'I have my two o'clock. Would you like to come with me and see Janine?'

WE FOLLOWED THE ROUTE we knew, but it was novel in Dad's car. We were driving fast. I looked out for cops, and she slowed down at the speed traps, the rhythms of the drive now reflex after years of rushing to get places on time. We drove to her favourite shopping mall, the one with Spanish tiles.

The bell on the door tinkled and Janine looked up from her magazine and came over to greet us. She was the only one there. Her acrylics clacked when she took my hands in hers and told me how sorry she was.

'Thank you,' I said. Janine said my mother had told her how good I was: staying with her at the house and taking care of things.

I looked at Mom, flattered to hear how she talked about me to others.

'I don't know where you found the strength,' Mom said. 'I've been barely getting by with the paperwork, and I keep thinking that we should arrange a memorial, but...'

Janine sat her down in a massage chair, saying 'One step at a time.'

'We'll figure it out,' I said.

She smiled at us. She looked so grateful.

Then Janine grabbed a pile of magazines and set me up in the massage chair next to my mother's. Janine filled a basin with hot water. My mother took off her shoes and submerged her feet. The magazines lay unopened in my lap as I watched Janine set to work on her. My mother's head tipped back. She shut her eyes. Janine scrubbed, kneaded, trimmed, and polished. Loving her felt easy when I saw her like this. Relaxing into pleasure. Sustained. Receptive to an act of care.

We went to pick up my cheque when we were done. As Mom waited for the woman at reception to return from the office, I wandered around the art centre's gallery. It was the same art but different. One of the painting classes had been themed to Moulin Rouge. The colours were muddled, brown, purple, and grey. The angle of the spine made the model seem as though she had been pieced together from parts of other women and had failed to reanimate. The elaborate undergarments seemed punitive. I wondered how the painter had learned to see, when he'd closed his eyes. If it was a choice or a reflex. On a table near the paintings was a twisting torso made of red clay. I recognized Fumiko's hand, the troublous curves. Not a figure study, not a nude, but a landscape of desire.

I TOOK THE KARMANN GHIA and my board and headed for the surfers' bay. There was no one on the road this time of night. The night was clear, the late-August moon large. I could even make out the lights on the island. I'd split the week between my apartment and here – not just to see Orly, I wanted to get to know my mother better and see Krit. He and I only really had the one thing in common, but it was enough – an interest in the sea. I didn't want to be afraid of the water. As I drove, I imagined paddling out and floating in the wake of the moon, communing with the stars. I could already feel the wave inside me, its swell and curve. The surf was loud as I came down the path, and when the waves pulled back, a sound that has always made me sad, I heard shrieks of joy and chatter.

There was a small group sitting by the fire lit in the fort. Krit saw me coming and waved. A woman offered me a beer. The can was half-covered in sand, which got in my teeth, even though I'd wiped the top off. I sat down. A wave rolled in, low and foaming over by the tide pools, the rocks tumbled as it pulled out. But the beach wasn't quite itself. There was something strange about the sandy shore. It was agitated, twitching and pulsing, like water at full boil. Nobody was surfing. I tried to make sense of the moonlight thrashing in the sand. Two women were ankle-deep in the silver, one held a bucket, the other buried her hands in the scrum. When she raised them up, her fists were full of fish. Grunion. They brought their catch to the fire and threw it on the grill. Krit handed me a fish and squeezed lemon on it.

I took my plate and broke away from the crowd for a closer look. The female fishes' heads stuck up, their round intent eyes, tails burrowed in the sand, laying their eggs. The males coiled their long, slender bodies around them. The water slid across it all, quieting the wriggling down, only to pull back again and reveal a frenzy. Orly would love this, I thought. This wild nature, so clear about what it wants. I called her. 'I'm eating grunion in the middle of a grunion run... How do they taste? A little sour.'

'Not like ecstasy,' she said, laughing. 'You know, I've never seen a fish orgy.'

I gave her directions, and as we were hanging up, I heard Orly say: 'Wait.'

I waited.

She said: 'I want you to count each wave until I come.'

So I started counting:

'One...'

Acknowledgements

This novel is indebted to many writers, artists, and activists, and their work. It would also not exist without the communities I've been lucky enough to be a part of.

Many resources have shaped this novel, too many to list here, but the following should be acknowledged. In thinking about landscape: Mary Austin's *The Land of Little Rain*, Jonathan White's *Tides: The Science and Spirit of the Ocean*. Womanhood and blood: Helen King's *The Disease of Virgins* and Leonard Shlain's *The Alphabet Versus the Goddess*. Sex work and BDSM: Pat Califia's 'Whoring in Utopia' and Guy Baldwin's *Ties That Bind*.

The epigraph is from Camille Paglia, 'The Return of Carry Nation: Catharine MacKinnon and Andrea Dworkin' (*Playboy*, October 1992). The scenes with the Director riff on *Alfred Hitchcock Presents*. The quotes from *Superman* are taken from *Superman*, Vol. 1 #261: *Slave of Star Sapphire*, copyright Cary Bates and DC Comics. The quotation from the composer when Echo is at Hollywood and Highland is taken from Erika Rothenberg's permanent public art project *The Road to Hollywood*.

I am forever grateful to everyone I came to know through those special houses I'll refer to here as CdS and HoB, where I was taught new ways of loving that set my life on a particular course. (Thank you for opening the door, S and S.) Thank you, John O'Connor, Rachael Allen, Madeleine LaRue, Lauren Marks, Anne Meadows, Mui Poopoksakul, Ryan Ruby, and Andrea Scrima for reading, listening, and keeping me up when doubt, nerves, and fear were weighing me down. Thank you, Janet Fitch, Noel Riley Fitch, and Amy Friedman for the lessons in writing and the writing life. Thank you, John Freeman and Ellah Allfrey, for bringing me into an environment where I learned so much about reading and writing, and, ultimately, found out what kind of writer I wanted to be. Thank you, Marina Penalva, without whose encouragement and deadline-setting I'd probably still be sitting on an unfinished manuscript, and who, along with Maria Cardona and Anna Soler-Pont, sent this book into the world. Thank you, Sharmaine Lovegrove, for the inspiration, support, and friendship throughout this long journey, for being the first to say yes, and, along with Alana Wilcox, for helping me find the shape of this novel. Alana and Sharmaine, thank you both for a dreamy editing experience. To Bill Vogel, Margot Vogel, and Marsela McGrane for your love and support, no matter what. And especially my mother Margot, the most inspiring reader I know. To Gaby Koeppe and Anne Voss for the gift of space. To David Hermann Fox, the fiercest protector of my heart, my time, and so much more.

Saskia Vogel is from Los Angeles and lives in Berlin, where she works as a writer and Swedish-to-English literary translator. She has written on power and sexuality for publications such as the *Paris Review Daily*, the *White Review, Sight & Sound*, and the *Offing*. Previously, she worked as *Granta* magazine's publicist and as an editor at the AVN Media Network, where she reported on pornography and adult pleasure products.

Typeset in Whitman and Neutra.

Printed at the Coach House on bpNichol Lane in Toronto, Ontario, on Zephyr Antique Laid paper, which was manufactured, acid-free, in Saint-Jérôme, Quebec, from second-growth forests. This book was printed with vegetable-based ink on a 1973 Heidelberg KORD offset litho press. Its pages were folded on a Baumfolder, gathered by hand, bound on a Sulby Auto-Minabinda and trimmed on a Polar single-knife cutter.

Edited by Alana Wilcox and Sharmaine Lovegrove
Designed by Alana Wilcox and Crystal Sikma
Cover by Ingrid Paulson
Cover image, *Sleepy*, by Rozenn Le Gall

Coach House Books
80 bpNichol Lane
Toronto ON M5S 3J4
Canada

416 979 2217
800 367 6360

mail@chbooks.com
www.chbooks.com